Jalal Had No Idea What It Was.

Maybe it was the stiffness that took over her body, or the pulse going haywire in her throat, or the fear of discovery in her eyes.

Or it was all of that and a thousand other instantaneous, involuntary signs that coalesced and painted a picture worth a thousand confessions.

It all added up to one thing. One thing that lodged in his mind with the force of an ax. Something devastating.

The truth.

Lujayn's child was his.

Dear Reader,

Jalal Aal Shalaan, the hero of *The Sheikh's Claim,* was an enigma to me as I started writing his story. He's already appeared in most of his brothers' stories, but he's been the one who wouldn't show me more than what he showed the world—the devil-may-care facade of a prince with the world at his feet. Then, in *The Sheikh's Redemption,* his twin Haidar's book, we finally got hints that not all was as it seemed with this knight of the desert. He was the "wolf" to Haidar's "lion," and their radical differences had torn them apart. By the end of that book, it seemed their lifelong rivalry and conflict were resolved, and they were finding their way back to their childhood closeness.

But the twins are still competing for the throne of Azmahar. And Jalal wants it with a burning passion. He believes he has nothing else to look forward to. His siblings and father have found their soul mates and are happy with their families, and he feels left out, aimless and alone. He believes he'll always be that way, for the only woman he could ever want is lost to him.

Is it any wonder, when she reappears in Azmahar, that his pursuit of Lujayn is relentless, even when her rejection is as single-minded? And that was before he discovers a secret that will make it even more unquestionable that he *will* claim her as his own, for life.

I loved writing Jalal and Lujayn's story as they came from totally opposite life situations—a prince and a pauper in love-story format—and not only met halfway but became one. I hope you enjoy reading their story as much as I enjoyed writing it!

I love to hear from readers, so please email me at oliviagates@gmail.com and connect with me on Facebook at my fan page Olivia Gates Author, on Goodreads and on Twitter @OliviaGates.

Thanks for reading!

Olivia

OLIVIA GATES

THE SHEIKH'S CLAIM

HARLEQUIN®
entertain, enrich, inspire™

ISBN-13: 978-0-373-73196-1

THE SHEIKH'S CLAIM

Books by Olivia Gates

Harlequin Desire

Silhouette Desire

*Throne of Judar
†The Castaldini Crown
**Pride of Zohayd
††Desert Knights

Other titles by this author available in ebook format.

OLIVIA GATES

has always pursued creative passions such as singing and handicrafts. She still does, but only one of her passions grew gratifying enough, consuming enough, to become an ongoing career—writing.

She is most fulfilled when she is creating worlds and conflicts for her characters, then exploring and untangling them bit by bit, sharing her protagonists' every heart-wrenching heartache and hope, their every heart-pounding doubt and trial, until she leads them to an indisputably earned and gloriously satisfying happy ending.

When she's not writing, she is a doctor, a wife to her own alpha male and a mother to one brilliant girl and one demanding Angora cat. Visit Olivia at www.oliviagates.com.

To my endlessly patient and supportive husband.
Thank you for being there for me always.
Love you, always.

One

Twenty-seven months ago

"So you managed to get away with murder this time."

Jalal Aal Shalaan frowned at the words he'd spoken aloud.

He was standing at the door of an opulent sitting room in one of the most breathtaking manors in the Hamptons, where he'd been received for years as an esteemed guest. He'd thought he'd never set foot in here again because of the woman who stood with her back to him. The woman who was now lady of the manor.

Lujayn Morgan. His ex-lover.

She'd been picking up letters from an antique marble table when his words had hit her. After a start, she'd frozen midmotion.

His own body was tense all over, too. His fists and jaw were clenched, his every muscle bunched, buzzing.

B'haggej' jaheem—by hell, why had he said that?

He hadn't intended to show her any hostility. Or any emotions at all—he'd thought he'd had none left. He'd come here for one reason. To see her without the lust that had blinded him for the four-year duration of their affair. He was here for closure, something she'd robbed him of when she'd stormed out of his life, giving him no chance to defend himself, to negotiate, leaving him wrestling with shock then rage and groping for explanations.

But he'd thought the resolution he was seeking was strictly intellectual. He'd thought he'd properly recovered during the two years since she'd walked out on him, working through his feelings until nothing remained but cold curiosity and mental aversion.

So he'd been deluding himself. What he'd felt for her, though it had reversed in nature, had remained as fierce.

He'd always presented the world with a devil-may-care facade. It was partly his nature and partly defensive. Having Sondoss, the notorious queen of Zohayd for a mother, and Haidar, the enigma who'd tormented him since childhood for a twin, made defenses necessary. They were the only ones who had ever managed to crack his control. Then had come Lujayn.

He was still vulnerable to the mere sight of her. And she hadn't even faced him yet.

Then she did.

Air deserted his lungs, heartbeats started to thunder.

Her beauty had always been mesmerizing. Her Middle Eastern and Irish genes conspired to create the personification of the best of both worlds. By the time she'd left him, brand names were starting to compete to have her willowy grace showcase their products, and makeup lines wanted that unforgettable face with those one-of-a-kind eyes to smolder at consumers out of their glossy ads.

But throughout their affair, she'd shed weight continuously. It had alarmed then angered him that her obsession with getting ahead in her career had blinded her to how she was harming herself to achieve a perfection she already possessed.

But the gaunt woman she'd been at the end of their affair had disappeared. In her place was the epitome of health and femininity with swells and dips that not even her severe black suit could tame, and had everything male in him roaring to life.

Marriage had been *very* good to her. Marriage to a man he'd once considered a good friend. A man who'd died less than two years after the wedding. A man whom he'd just more or less accused her of killing.

She inclined her head as she straightened, the movement emphasizing the elegance of her swan neck, the perfection of her raven chignon-wrapped head.

Her cool tranquility was a superb act, but her shock registered in something beyond her acting abilities. The pupils of uncanny irises, as silvery as the meaning of her name did that thing that had enthralled him when she was agitated or aroused, expanding and shrinking, giving the illusion that her eyes where emitting bursts of light.

The need to look closer into those eyes propelled him forward. Then words he hadn't known he'd been thinking, taunts that segued from his opening salvo, spilled from his lips.

"Not that I'm surprised. You've managed to fool the most suspicious and shrewd people I know, including myself. It shouldn't come as any surprise that not even New York's Finest were a match for your cunning."

"What are you doing here?"

Her voice jolted through him. Once a caress of crimson passion, it had filled with dark echoes, deepening its effect.

She shook her head as if exasperated with the inanity of her own question. "Scratch that. How did you get in here?"

He stopped two feet away, though every cell was screaming for him to keep going until he'd pressed his every inch to hers. Like when they'd been lovers. When she'd always met him more than halfway, impetuous, tempestuous...

Cursing inwardly, he shoved his hands in his pockets in feigned nonchalance. "Your housekeeper let me in."

She shook her head again, as if finding his answer ridiculous. Then her eyes widened with harsh accusation. "You intimidated her!"

Something twisted in his gut. In the past, she'd made him believe she thought he walked on water. Now the first thing that occurred to her was that he'd done something reprehensible. Worse, criminal.

But why would that upset him? He'd long accepted that her early adoration had been an act. One she hadn't been able to maintain once she'd suspected it wouldn't fulfill her purpose. Though he should marvel that it had taken over two years before she'd begun to slip, for instances of discord to accumulate.

He'd still refused to see that for what it was, pure manipulation. Instead, had assigned it all to the stress of her competitive job and the provocation of the dominant personality he became with her. He'd thought friction had only fueled their already incendiary relationship, had reveled in it to the point of instigating it on occasion. He'd misguided himself so thoroughly, that final explosive confrontation had utterly shocked him.

But after two years of dissecting the past, he now saw it clearly. He'd dismissed all evidence of the truth to maintain the illusion because he couldn't live without her passion. Or so he'd thought. He had. Hadn't he?

She now pulled herself to her full statuesque height, six

feet in her two-inch heels, her pose confrontational. "You might have scared Zahyah, but you must have forgotten all about me if you thought your arm-twisting tactics would work. You can walk out as you walked in, under your own power, or I'm calling security. Or better still, the police."

He flicked away her threat, his blood heating with the challenge and ardor she'd always ignited in him with a glance, a word. "What would you tell them? That your housekeeper let me in without consulting you and left you alone with me in an empty mansion?" Any other time he would have recommended the housekeeper be sternly chastised for such a breach of protocol and security. For now he was only glad she'd acted as she had. "On questioning, she'd swear there'd been no intimidation of any sort. As one of your mother's former colleagues, it was only natural for Zahyah to let me in."

"You mean because as my mother's former colleague, Zahyah was one of *your* mother's servants, too?"

He stiffened at the mention of his mother. The knowledge of her conspiracy to depose his father, King Atef, and remove his half brothers from succession to the throne of Zohayd was a skewer constantly turning inside him.

But Lujayn knew nothing of the conspiracy. No one but he and his siblings and father did. They'd been keeping it a secret at all costs until they resolved it. And resolution would come only when they discovered where his mother had hidden the Pride of Zohayd jewels. It was a backward and infuriating situation, one dictated by legend and now enforced by law—possession of the jewels conferred the right to rule Zohayd. Instead of calling for whoever had stolen them to be punished, Zohayd's people would decree that his father and his heirs, who had "lost" them, were unworthy of the throne. The belief that the jewels "sought" to be possessed by whoever deserved to rule the kingdom was unshakable.

But even when threatened with life imprisonment, his mother wouldn't confess to their location. All she'd told him and Haidar was that she would continue to destroy their father and brothers from her prison, that when the throne became Haidar's, with him as his crown prince, they would thank her.

He shook away the gnawing of ongoing frustration, leveling his gaze at the current cause of it. "I mean that Zahyah, as an Azmaharian who spent years in the royal palace of Zohayd—"

"As a virtual slave to your mother—as was mine."

The knot in his gut grew tighter as yet another of his mother's crimes sank its shame into him.

Ever since the exposure of Sondoss's conspiracy, they'd been realizing the full extent of her transgressions. *Slave* might be an exaggeration, but from recent findings, it had become evident she'd mistreated her servants. Lujayn's mother, as her "lady-in-waiting," seemed to have borne the brunt of her ruthless caprice. But Badreyah had left his mother's service as soon as Lujayn had left him. Seemed she could afford to when Lujayn had married Patrick McDermott.

That was probably one reason Lujayn had married him. Not that it made him any less bitter about it. She should have told him if she'd known Badreyah had been suffering at his mother's hands. He should have been the one she'd gone to for help.

He answered her cold fury with his own. "Whatever views Zahyah holds of my mother, she evidently still considers me her prince. She welcomed me in accordingly."

"Don't tell me you think people really buy this Prince of Two Kingdoms crap."

Her sneer had blood surging to his head. As half-Azmaharian half-Zohaydan princes, he and Haidar had been dubbed that. He couldn't speak for Haidar, but *he'd* always felt like a prince of neither kingdom. In Zohayd he was cut off from succession for being of impure stock. In Azmahar... well, he could count the reasons that no one there should consider him their prince.

The grandiose slogan that had been plastered over them from birth had always felt—as she'd pithily put it—like crap.

But then their mother decided to make it a reality. She was out to mangle and reform the region in order to do so.

He exhaled. "Whatever I am or am not, Zahyah welcomed me, and so did your guards before her. I've been welcomed here enough times that they didn't think twice of continuing the practice."

"You conned them using a defunct relationship with Patrick—"

"Who's no longer with us, thanks to you." He cut her off, the bile of pent-up anger welling again. "But you didn't prepare for developments as I thought you would. You didn't make allowance for my reappearance, didn't revoke my standing invitation."

"Like I would a vampire's, huh? Though one would be preferable to you since you're a *soul* sucker. And you're harder to banish. But I'll rectify that oversight right now."

He caught her arm as she strode past, felt awareness fork in his body. He gritted his teeth against the response, kept his breathing shallow so her scent—that of jasmine-scented twilights and pleasure-drenched nights—didn't trigger full-blown arousal.

"Don't bother. This delightful visit won't be repeated."

She jerked her arm free of his loose grasp. "It won't even start. You have some nerve coming here, after what you've done."

She was referring to his business clashes with Patrick,

which had resulted in major losses to them both. More damage *she'd* caused.

He misunderstood her on purpose. "I'm not the one who dumped you and married one of your best friends, only to turn her against you."

"You give Patrick too little credit if you think I influenced his decision to cut all business ties with you."

"You'd influence the devil himself. And we both know Patrick had too much angel in him. He was the perfect prey for the black widow you turned out to be."

Her eyes swept him from head to toe in disdain. "Listen, Jalal, cut the cloak-and-dagger melodrama. If you traveled across the world just to accuse me of overdosing my husband, you accomplished that with your opening statement. Don't be redundant as well as unfeeling and overbearing. You can now go back to your sand-infested, backward region to wallow in your unearned power."

Heat splashed in his chest. Not because her views insulted him, but because she had them at all. Disappointment only intensified his reaction to her, sent blood roaring to his loins.

His lips twisted with grim humor. "You were always a spitfire, yet you never spoke this brazenly to me."

"You just never bothered to listen. Not that that was a privilege you reserved for me. Your Exalted Highness didn't consider anyone worth listening to. But you're partially right. I was once guilty of embellishing my attitude and opinion of you. I'm not the person I was anymore."

"You're *exactly* the person you always were. But now that you're an heiress to an empire worth billions, you believe you have the luxury of showing me your true face and the clout to take me on."

Her eyes grew ridiculing. "That's not why I don't have to suppress my abhorrence of you and all you stand for anymore. But since I'm not inclined to explain my reasons, thanks for coming."

Thanks?

"I've been seething for two years that I didn't let it all out when I last saw you. Thanks for giving me the chance to get it off my chest. Now, since you've done what you've come to do, and indulged your evidently long-repressed desire to call me names—"

"But that's not what I've come to do." Before she could lob back something caustic, and without willing himself to, he dragged her to him, slamming her against his now burning body. "And that's certainly not the desire I've long repressed."

A hot sound of protest escaped her. He bent, caught it in his lips. He snatched in air laden with her breath, let it storm through him, uprooting the restraints he'd long placed on his senses. He let the feel of her invade his control, tear it away. Her taste eddied in his system, hurtling him back to their nights of delirium.

"No matter what you hate about me, you always loved this." He poured the words into her open-from-shock mouth, his lips gliding over her plump ones, pushing them farther apart, unable to wait to plunge inside her warmth and welcome. "You craved it. My touch, my hunger, my pleasures. Whatever else was pretense, this was real. Still is."

"It isn't…" Her words caught in her throat as soon as her lips moved against his. They trembled before they clung to his flesh.

It had always been like this. One touch had been all it took to ignite them, to start the chain reaction to the mindlessness and ecstasy of their overriding need for each other.

"Yes, Lujayn. It still is. This all-consuming need that ignites between us and only the other can satisfy."

Her breath hitched as it mingled with his, tumbled from

her on a ragged moan of arousal, as his tongue sought her concession. She gave it in a blatant seeking of her own, delighting him in her taste, her response. But at the first rub of slick flesh on flesh, a jolt of pleasure electrified both their bodies, made her start, try to escape the deepening intimacy. The move only had her teeth grazing his lips, tearing a groan from his depths, igniting her response again, her body involuntarily arching into his, their lips fusing again, sending his senses roaring for more.

He walked her back to the nearest wall, pressed against her lushness, imprinted her silent demand with his. "Tell me you have lain at night like I have, burning to have me again, take your fill of me. Tell me you have been going insane like I have. Tell me that you remembered all that we shared the moment I showed up, that even as your lips antagonized me, all you really wanted was for me to fill you, ride you, assuage the ache that maddens you."

He raised his head, looked down at her to get her confirmation. He got it.

She still wanted him. She'd never stopped.

It showed in the burning desire and dismay in her eyes. Whatever she'd been telling herself since she'd left him, her explosive response to him had forced her to face facts.

Holding her eyes, still seeking her affirmation, he scooped her into his arms. She clung to him, gave him more proof of her consent.

His heart almost uprooted itself in his chest with relief and urgency as he almost ran with her filling his arms, her eagerness tugging him deeper into mindlessness. It was only when he lowered her onto a king-size bed that he realized that his feet had propelled him to the master suite.

He came down half on top of her, stopped her roaming hands, stretched her arms above her head, capturing her wrists in one hand. The other slid down her face, her neck, skimmed over her breasts. Then, holding her gaze clouded with feverish desire, he leaned in, capturing her lips at the same moment he snapped open her jacket.

She gasped and turned her head as if suddenly shy, making his kisses trail over the hot velvet of her cheek. At the first suckle of his lips on her earlobe, she arched up, bringing her luxurious breasts rubbing against his chest, shuddering hard at the electrifying contact, intensifying it.

He rose to let her expression guide him to his next action. She stared up at him, her eyes emitting those hypnotic bursts, her breath choppy, her nipples pushing through her bra and blouse.

Satisfaction spread at the explicitness of her response, heightened as a gasp of disappointment escaped her when he sat up. His smile placated her as he shrugged away his jacket. Then, analyzing every iota of expression in her eyes' eloquent depths, he slowly, so slowly, unbuttoned his shirt.

His deliberateness gave her time and opportunity to take action if she didn't want this to go further. Gave him the luxury of studying her as she watched him expose his body to her. The body she'd worshipped for four years, laid her indelible brand over every inch. He reveled in each of her nuances as hunger and memories flooded her eyes, igniting them, swelling her lips, staining her cheeks.

"Isn't this what you've been burning for?" Her nod was drugged, her eyes glazing over as silent confession strummed her voluptuous body, shook her lips. He brought her hands pressing against his flesh, one over his thundering heart, the other over his abdomen, which quivered with need. When her volition took over, he invited her to go lower, groaned long and deep as she shaped him, cupped him, in trembling greed.

He hissed his torment, encouraging her, his mind unraveling with the sheer power and pleasure of her longed-for touch, and that of her desire. "Feel me, Lujayn. Take what you've always wanted. Enjoy me, revel in me. Devour me with your hunger like you used to, *ya'yooni'l feddeyah*."

A jolt racked her at hearing him call her one of his favorite endearments for her, *my silver eyes*. Their intoxicated cast deepened until they were the color of twilight in Zohayd. Snatched breaths escaped her lips as she explored him with intensifying boldness, each ending on a fractured moan. His intention to draw this out until she begged for him dwindled with each siren sound. But it was when she squeezed her eyes shut and agonized enjoyment gripped her face as she roamed him, that it vanished.

On a growled oath, he removed her hands from his rock-hard flesh. Before he moved over her, she jerked, as if coming out of a trance and scrambled up. "Jalal, we have to stop...."

He went still. "Tell me why."

She squeezed her eyes again. "Patrick..."

He caught her head in both hands, made her open her eyes. "Is dead. And you and I are not. But we're not alive, either. Tell me you've been able to truly *live*...without this...." He took her lips again as he moved his hard length over her until her tension dissolved, into seeking surrender, her body straining against his. He tore away his lips from hers to rise above her on extended arms. "Tell me you have known any real pleasure or satisfaction since me. Say you don't crave me as much as I crave you and I will go."

The truth blared in her eyes, but she still said, "Craving is not everything...."

"It's enough." He dug his fingers into her prim chignon, setting her raven silk free, burying his face in its luxury. "It's what we have, what we need, what we can't fight."

She pulled up his head by his hair. "It won't change a thing."

She held his focus. She was setting terms for this encounter. That it would only be physical? Or that it would be a one-off?

He refused to concede. "It will. It will stop this need from gnawing us hollow. Now admit it. You've been dying to have me again as I've been dying to have you. You'll give me everything as you always did, let me give you everything you've always begged for, everything we've always had together."

After a long moment, she nodded. Then with sooty lashes lowered to hide her expression, she dragged his mouth back to hers.

He growled his relief inside her as her tongue tangled with his, dueling, demanding, allowing him all the licenses he needed, taking her pleasure from him as she always did, her fervor and boldness intensifying his, her hunger and warmth and taste flowing in his lifeblood.

One hand harnessed her by her hair's tether as one of hers did him by his as he undid her blouse and skirt, swept them off her velvet flesh. Her other hand trembled at his zipper as he snapped open her bra, spilling her breasts. He swallowed her cry of relief, of spiking arousal, as he settled his aching flesh on top of hers, rubbing against her until she begged.

"Do everything to me, Jalal. Fill me, ride me now, *now*."

He rose to tear her panties off her hips, probe her satiny folds. His fingers slid in her flowing need, until she undulated against him in a frenzy. When he couldn't stand one more heartbeat outside her heat and yearning, she clamped her thighs around his back, writhing in the grips of the same fever to merge. Then he plunged inside her.

She screamed with the shock of his invasion. She was as impossibly tight as ever, their fit still almost unmanageable, their pleasure excruciating. She arched, smashing herself against him with the mindless need for his domination.

Overwhelmed with feeling, his girth gripped inside the molten pleasure that was her essence, he groaned her name and withdrew, only to plunge again, then again, forging deeper with every penetration. His escalations rocked her beneath him, wringing sharper cries from her depths. She met his thrusts, strengthening them, her demands for him to give it all to her tearing away any restraint he'd still clung to.

Their coupling was primal, savage. They groped and bit and thrust in ever-roughening abandon, nothing existing but the need to soothe the pangs that had long maddened them, to burn in a conflagration of release.

The first clench of her orgasm hit him like a sledgehammer. Her core clamped around his shaft with such force, he tore his lips from hers to roar at the unendurable spike in pleasure. Then she heaved beneath him, her intimate flesh tightening around his erection, singeing him with the rush of her satisfaction, wrenching his own from the depth of his loins. His body felt as if it was detonating with the force of his own climax as he released inside her, feeling he was pouring his life force into her.

Ecstasy finally relinquished its merciless grip and her strangled cries died into whimpers as aftershocks sparked and lurched through both of them.

He sank on top of her, oblivious to anything but her body cushioning him, her chaotic heartbeats echoing his as their systems struggled to recover from the exertion of their explosive lovemaking.

He might have slept. Or passed out. For a minute. Or an hour. All he knew was that he was coming back with a start into a body that was leaden with an excess of fulfillment. Then a move beneath him had him jerking up. *Lujayn*. He must have crushed her.

He groaned, then louder with the ache of separation, as he uncoupled from her with great regret. He bent to kiss her, but she scooted away from his touch. His heart clenched as she swayed up and sat at the edge of the bed, long hair tumbled, her body still and stiff.

He was reaching a caressing hand to her again when she turned her face and the look in her eyes halted the gesture of tenderness in midmotion. And that was before she spoke.

"I hate you, Jalal. When I've never hated anyone. So consider this the validation or the goodbye or whatever sex you think I owed you. It's never happening again."

She got up like an automaton. In seconds she disappeared inside the bathroom.

He stared at the closed door, heart booming, mind churning.

One thing that had been erased had been resurrected. His confidence in his ownership of her body. If he went after her now, he'd have her begging for him again. But her antipathy seemed to be real. He had no idea what he had done to earn it. But whatever *she* thought he had done might change everything. It might explain why she'd left him.

It was almost an hour before she exited the bathroom glowing, remote and dressed. He'd also dressed. He knew their mindless interlude should not be repeated. Not until he knew what was going on.

He stood there as she stopped before him, eyes devoid of expression. "I'm sorry I said I hate you. It's not true."

His heart unfurled from the tight knot it had become, the broken pieces mending. Something warm fluttered inside it as he moved closer.

Her next words froze it solid, shot it down like a bullet would a bird in flight.

"It's worse than that. I hate *myself* when I'm with you. I hate what I do, what I think, what I feel. What I *am*. Patrick taught me that I'm better than that—that I don't have to ever feel this way again. I was certain I'd never do this. But you're like an incurable disease. One exposure, and I relapse. There's only one way I'll stop being reinfected. I won't let you come near me again. If you try, I'll make you regret it."

The lash of her antipathy sliced open the dam of his accumulated, if briefly forgotten, bitterness.

He moved away from her, as if to escape the searing disappointment, heard himself taunting, "You mean more than I already regret coming here and exposing myself to *your* virulence again? Not possible. So save your threats and theatrics, Lujayn. It will be a snowy day in my 'backward region' before I come near you again."

He didn't only regret coming after her—he despised his stupidity for being unable to hate her, even now, for succumbing to his weakness, taking her right in her marital bed, then not being the one who came to his senses first, or at all.

At the door he turned, and the look on her face had his heartache boiling over. It wasn't just over, she didn't only hate him now—she always had.

It had been an illusion, a sham.

More harshness spilled from his lips, the only shield he found so the icy shards of her rejection wouldn't hack his heart to pieces all over again. "Thanks, by the way. You gave me exactly what I came for. The certainty that you're not worth another thought. *Now* I can delete you from my memory."

He walked away then, the relief that this retaliation had provided already evaporating, despondence seeping in its place, settling into his recesses. For it was another lie. No matter that he now knew nothing they'd shared had been real, he knew the memory of her would never relinquish its hold over him....

Two

"...the memory of this day will burn bright for the rest of my days, with the blessing and wonder of your love and belief, your very existence. I, Haidar Aal Shalaan, pledge my life to you, Roxanne, owner of my heart..."

Jalal hit Pause, his chest tight as he watched the power of love radiating from the two faces frozen on the screen.

He'd never believed in miracles. But there was no denying he'd watched one unfold in real time. Had been replaying it on video over and over again. His twin's wedding ceremony. He'd watched that specific part, when they'd made their un-rehearsed vows, for the umpteenth time. Today.

Each time had only ratcheted up his reaction to the sight of Haidar staring with such profound adoration into the eyes of his weeping bride, of hearing him, then her, commit to a lifetime of unity and allegiance, body and soul.

He *was* fiercely happy for both of them. The twin who felt like an extension of his own life force, and the woman who felt of his own flesh and blood, too. But seeing them, *feeling* them, bound together in abiding love forever, inflicted something besides joy. It made him feel even more acutely that gaping emptiness in his core. One he knew would never be filled.

He'd once thought he'd had a chance of having something approaching what Haidar and Roxanne had. With Lujayn, the one woman he'd wanted with all he had. But even when they'd been lost to passion in each other's arms, he'd felt something missing. Now he knew what it was. *That.* That connection. That alliance. That totality of acceptance, agreement and appreciation.

The extent of the deficiency had been driven home to him during the past years as his brothers had found their soul mates. But it had taken Haidar and Roxanne to solidify the realization. He'd now seen and felt what completeness was like.

He hadn't had anything like it with Lujayn. But then how could he have? It took two to progress to that level of intimacy. She'd been unwilling to move beyond a certain threshold. She hadn't wanted intimacy, she'd wanted wealth and status.

He saw that now. At the time he'd thought any issues had been due to the intermittent nature of their relationship, dictated by their hectic schedules and living on different sides of the world. But the truth had been that, beyond sex, she hadn't really wanted *him.* She'd only wanted him to propose.

He'd bet she would have kept trying if another opportunity, almost as big a catch, hadn't presented itself.

He hit Stop. The screen went black—as black as his thoughts.

He wouldn't see it again. There was no point in replaying the living, breathing example of what he'd never have. He'd have a lifetime of experiencing it in real life.

He rose and threw down the remote. It took him seconds to get his bearings, to remember where this sitting room opened onto the veranda. He'd rented so many houses in the past two years that he regularly woke up not knowing immediately where he was, or even in which country.

Ever since his mother's conspiracy had been exposed and the scandal had rocked the region, he'd been roaming the globe. His father and half brothers, Amjad, Harres and Shaheen, insisted that no one associated Haidar and him to her crimes. But he felt tainted by them anyway. He'd felt worse when he'd clashed with Haidar over that mess, and ended up placing the lion's share of the blame on him. He'd driven Haidar to say he felt he no longer had a twin.

That breach *had* been resolved, thankfully, and he no longer felt sundered forever from his other half. But though he felt whole now that their relationship was regaining the closeness they'd once shared as children, that wholeness was still…hollow.

He walked across the marble-spread veranda and stopped at the cut-stone balustrade, looking out at the desert to a horizon that seemed farther away than ever.

What was he doing here?

Why was he trying to claim the throne of this land?

So it was up for grabs after the now former king of Azmahar, his maternal uncle, had abdicated after a public outcry and all his heirs had met with the same rejection. Just as his mother had almost destroyed Zohayd, her family had taken Azmahar to the edge of destruction, too. He'd thought he'd be lumped in with his maternal family as the last people Azmahar would want near the throne again. So he'd been shocked when those representing a third of the kingdom's population had demanded he be their candidate. They'd insisted he wasn't tainted by his family's history and had the power and experience to save Azmahar. Even his Aal Munsoori blood was an asset, since people still considered the bloodline their rightful monarchs. But he had the potent advantage of mixing it with the Aal Shalaan blood, which would win them back their vital ally, Zohayd.

Still, why was *he* running for the throne? So he knew he was qualified for the position. But he also knew that he could swim among sharks, literally. He'd done it before. But that didn't mean he should—and running for the position of king in such a chaotic land was worse than braving shark-infested waters. Not to mention the minefield of being pitted against his twin *and* his former-best-friend-turned-nemesis, Rashid.

He could find one real reason. Because if he didn't do this, what else was there to do?

He'd exiled himself from Zohayd, had been performing from afar the royal duties his brothers hadn't taken over in his absence. He'd installed such an efficient system to run his business empire, it took him only a few hours a day to orchestrate its almost self-perpetuating success. And he had no personal life. Apart from a few good-but-not-close friends, he had no one.

Sure, his family insisted he had them, and he supposed he did, in the big-picture sense, but on a daily basis? His family back in Zohayd he seldom saw. And he now had his twin back, but only in an emotional sense. As a newlywed and another candidate for the throne, Haidar had no real time for him.

No wonder he felt empty. As vacant as this desert, with as nonexistent a possibility for change.

An insistent noise broke the stillness of his surroundings. He frowned down at its origin. His cell phone.

It took him seconds to recognize the ring, one he'd assigned to a specific person. Fadi Aal Munsoori. A distant cousin, and the head of his security and his campaign for the throne.

Though Fadi came from the one branch of Jalal's family on his mother's side that he considered "family," Fadi himself had never considered he had any relation to the former royal family of Azmahar. Fadi's father had maintained marginal relations with them, but Fadi had renounced the relationship completely, not to mention publicly and viciously. The moment they'd been deposed, he'd pounced on the tribes he had influence over, had been the one who'd orchestrated their nomination of Jalal for king.

But even as the one he trusted with his life, his business, his campaign and even his secrets, Fadi had never accepted Jalal's efforts to form a more personal relationship. Jalal insisted he was foremost a friend, but Fadi behaved like a knight of old with Jalal as his liege. He only ever called him when there was something urgent to convey or to discuss.

He almost wished Fadi would hit him with something huge to deal with, to get him out of this vacuum.

"Fadi, so good to hear from you."

Not one to indulge in niceties, Fadi got to the point, his deep voice pouring its usual solemn gravity into Jalal's ear.

"Considering you have not renewed my orders concerning this matter, or asked about any developments in the past two years, you may not be interested in what I have to tell you. But I decided to let you know in case you still are."

Jalal's gut tightened. This didn't sound like something that concerned his business, his personal safety or his campaign. There was only one other thing Fadi had ever taken care of for him. One person he'd entrusted him with keeping tabs on. Lujayn.

It seemed he hadn't groaned her name mentally but out loud, for Fadi said, "Yes, this is about Lujayn Morgan."

The desert wind suddenly stirred, as if in response to the questions and temptations that stormed through him.

He'd been holding himself back with all he had so that he wouldn't "renew Fadi's orders" or "ask about any developments." And he'd succeeded. At least he'd managed not to seek her out, or learn news of her, thereby renewing his exposure and losing any hard-won closure.

The sane thing to do now was to leave Fadi certain that his orders concerning her were at an end. That he was not to even report any information that came his way by accident.

At his prolonged silence, Fadi exhaled. "I apologize for presuming you would be interested."

And he did the one insane thing. Heartbeat spiraling out of control, he growled, *"B'haggej' jaheem, ya rejjal,* just *tell* me."

His bark silenced Fadi instead. Fadi, like everyone else, believed Jalal was the epitome of sangfroid. While this was mostly true, control and Lujayn had always been mutually exclusive.

He could almost hear Fadi's miss-nothing mind clicking on the new conclusion before he finally said, "She is back in Azmahar."

"Did you think I wouldn't find out you were in Azmahar?"

Lujayn pulled away the cell phone to groan at hearing a voice she'd come back here hoping to avoid.

Aliyah's.

She and Aliyah had once thought they were cousins, with both their fathers belonging to the Irish-American Morgan clan. But Aliyah's mother, Princess Bahiyah Aal Shalaan, had turned out to be her flesh and blood aunt, with Aliyah actually the daughter of now-ex-King Atef Aal Shalaan of

Zohayd from his American lover, and now new wife, Anna Beaumont.

It had been years since Aliyah had been declared an Aal Shalaan and become the wife of King Kamal Aal Masood and the queen of Judar. Quite a change from the minor royalty she'd been when Lujayn had known her.

But while their false family relationship had introduced them to each other, they had become true friends when Lujayn had followed Aliyah's footsteps in modeling. Aliyah had offered her unfailing guidance and priceless support, steered her from many a mess and hooked her up with the few people it was safe to know in that turbulent world.

Aliyah had also been the reason she'd met Jalal, back when they'd thought she was a cousin to them both. Now that they knew Aliyah was his half sister, there was an even bigger chance she might pull Lujayn into Jalal's orbit once more. That was why she'd been avoiding her. That and the fathomless joy Aliyah radiated ever since she'd gotten married.

"So what is an appropriate punishment for you, now that I've caught you in Azmahar unannounced?" Aliyah's vibrant voice teased.

Lujayn wasn't about to confess to the woman who'd shown her unforgettable kindness when she'd most needed it that she'd been avoiding her because she inadvertently made her feel bad about her life and because she didn't want to risk seeing Jalal.

So she told her what she felt, free of pettiness and anxieties. "I missed you, too, Aliyah."

Aliyah let out a laugh as clear and tinkling as crystal. "And here she is. The woman who knows just how to thwart me and still leave me with a smile on my face. You're more slippery than an eel, you know that? I hear it's an Azmaharian trait."

A smile pried Lujayn's stiff lips apart. It had been an end-less source of fun among them to compare notes on their "hybrid" nature. "Since I'm only half-Azmaharian, the trait must be diluted, so I can't be that slippery."

Aliyah hooted. "My dear, you're talking to a bona fide halfling. Being half-and-half only augments any traits we inherit from each side. Just ask Kamal."

And there it was. The woman was unable to form five consecutive sentences without leading back to her husband and love of her life.

She knew she was being pathetic, but it wasn't just hear-ing the wealth of love in Aliyah's voice. She'd seen them to-gether, alone and with their two children. Seeing and feeling that lion of a man's fierce love and devotion to Aliyah had been amazing, but it was also evidence that such passion existed—and that she would never have anything like it.

"So how long are you in Azmahar?" Aliyah interrupted her darkening thoughts. "Last time you were here was more than four years ago and you stayed less than four days."

"I don't know, Aliyah. It depends on my aunt's health."

"Suffeyah?" All levity left Aliyah's voice, alarm replac-ing it. "What's wrong with her?"

"She's been diagnosed with breast cancer."

"Oh, Lujayn, I'm so sorry. Bring her over to Judar. We have one of the best medical systems in the world, thanks to Kamal. I'll see to it that she has the best health care the kingdom can offer."

"I can't thank you enough for the offer, Aliyah, but I have to decline it. I tried to make her come to the States, but she refuses to leave her daughters behind for the months the treatments might take. One is a senior in high school and the other just had twins."

"I understand all too well putting your kids before yourself. But Azmahar isn't in good shape and I understand one of the sectors suffering most is health care."

Lujayn's heart constricted at Aliyah's words. "I know. But Aunt insists she'll take her chances with the medical care here like any other Azmaharian would. All I could do was arrange for a consult with some of the best doctors in the States. I'm flying them over in a couple days. We'll take it from there."

"That's great. And if what they recommend can't be carried out in Azmahar, I'll provide you with medicine, equipment and personnel. If she won't come to us, we'll bring the best of Judar to her."

"Oh, Aliyah, that is beyond anything I could have hoped for."

"But you didn't hope for anything, did you? You have this infuriating thing against a helping hand from a friend."

Lujayn exhaled. Aliyah was right. Being the daughter of a servant in the palace Aliyah had grown up in had been enough. She hadn't wanted to tip the balance of their situations more by accepting favors she'd be unable to repay. She'd only accepted Aliyah's help when Aliyah had insisted it was the fruit of her experience, nothing to do with her royal status.

Even now she had nothing of equal value to ever offer Aliyah. That made it impossible for her to be the recipient of favors that had everything to do with Aliyah's status.

"I can hear your mind churning, Lu," Aliyah said. "But since it's not you on the receiving end this time, it should ameliorate your allergic reaction. Now promise you won't say no, and you'll let me do what I can when needed."

She chuckled even as tears rushed to her eyes. "I forgot how well you know me, Aliyah. And about this pesky total recall of yours. *And* just how incredible you are." She sighed, swallowing the lump of emotion. "Thank you, and I promise."

"Good girl!" She could just see Aliyah's unbridled smile. "Now when will I see you?"

Ugh. Now she had to make another promise.

But why not? She knew it would be beyond either of them to keep this one. She doubted the queen of Judar would find it feasible to continue a friendship with someone of her background.

She exhaled. "As soon as we know more about the plans for Aunt, I'll call you to set up a girls' day out."

Aliyah whooped. "And I'm holding you to that."

After more chatting, Lujayn started to regain the fluency they'd once shared, until Aliyah had to rush to extract her daughter from a literally sticky mess and laughingly bade her adieu.

Lujayn collapsed on the nearest seat. If she was already coming apart, what would the next weeks or months here be like?

It was just her terrible luck to come back to Azmahar now, with Jalal on Azmaharian soil for the first time in years. She hated being in the same airspace as him. And Aliyah's call had made her feel as if his shadow was closer and darker than ever.

Which was moronic. Not only had he said he'd delete her from his memory, he had a throne to think of. Even if he hadn't, she'd be the last thing to cross his mind. She'd been the last thing he'd thought about or considered when she'd been his sex partner. She'd been one of many, after all.

He'd arranged their rendezvouses when it had been convenient for him, sometimes weeks apart, and no way had he suppressed his overriding libido that long. She'd spent the times apart alternating between a hell of doubt, and telling herself it was only her insecurities talking. But she'd seen and heard too much proof that instead of "storing his hunger to be expended on her luscious self" as he'd once claimed, he'd had a different body in his bed every night.

To her shame, that hadn't been what had finally made her walk away.

After all, he'd promised her nothing to justify her feeling bad, let alone betrayed.

Cursing herself for regurgitating those sordid memories, her eyes darted around the hotel suite. She'd reserved it for the coming weeks as it was within walking distance of the hospital so she'd be constantly available for her aunt.

She'd just come back from starting arrangements at the hospital. Just thinking of what lay ahead filled her with dread. No wonder Aliyah's call had shaken her. She was already in turmoil. And it had nothing to do with any other Aal Shalaan.

She rose and headed to the kitchenette to make a cup of herbal tea. She needed to be calm for the drive back to her aunt's at the outskirts of Durrat al Sahel. Traffic in the capital had gotten far worse than she remembered.

With the first sip from her hibiscus brew, a loud, melodious noise shattered the suite's silence. She gulped the hot liquid, scalded her tongue and choked.

She was coughing her lungs out when the noise went off again. A doorbell. She hadn't even realized the suite had one!

It must be housekeeping. And she hadn't thought of hanging a Do Not Disturb sign—she'd planned to stay only an hour.

She stalked to the door, flung it open, intending to let them in and herself out…and froze. Her heart did, too.

Filling the door, dwarfing her and causing the world to shrink, stood Jalal. The reason behind every tumult in her life since she'd laid eyes on him.

But he wasn't only that man. He was…more.

She'd once thought nothing could surpass him in beauty and magnificence. And nothing had. And during their affair, he'd proved only he could best his own standards. That six-foot-six broad-shouldered, divinely proportioned body she'd thought the epitome of manhood *had* kept maturing to godlike levels, as she'd had hands-on proof. Every day they'd had together had hewn his face further with the chisel of maturity and virility, manifesting his intelligence and sensuality and dominance in its every slash and angle and expression.

But something had happened to him since she'd last seen him two years ago. As if the darkness and danger she'd long suspected he'd hidden beneath the facade of graciousness and gorgeousness had manifested in his looks, emanated from his every nuance. It turned his beauty, his impact, from breathtaking to heartbreaking.

He was staring down at her as if he, too, was shocked to see her. When he was the one who'd almost given her a heart attack just by showing up.

After what felt like an hour of suspended thought and escalating distress, his whiskey-colored eyes narrowed, singeing her. Then his voice poured over her, feeling like a dip in lava.

"I said I'd delete you from my memory, but it appears there is no forgetting you without erasing it altogether. So I've decided to stop trying, to go all the way in the opposite direction. I now think my only cure is to revive every memory, to reenact every single intimacy we ever shared."

Three

Lujayn stood paralyzed as Jalal pushed past her. The door clicked closed, sounded like a gun going off at close range.

She still couldn't move. Speak. Breathe. Reactions deluged her as she watched him walk farther into the suite, memories and sensations and compulsions tangling, trapping her volition in their maze. It had always taken him just a look to neutralize her will, her sense of self-preservation.

And that he still retained the same influence over her, after all she'd suffered and lost and continued to struggle with because of him, made her spitting, foaming mad.

The moment he turned to face her, his eyes sweeping her in tranquil appreciation and intent, she seethed, "What the hell do you think you're doing? Get out."

"I will. At some point." His shoulders moved in a languid shrug. "But since it won't be now, how about saving your obligatory apoplectic tirade and getting on with discussing the particulars of my proposition?"

"How about I revive our first memory? Reenact the first 'intimacy' I shared with you?"

His wolf's eyes flared with remembrance as he walked back to her. "When I first saw you hiding behind Aliyah and watching me like a wary, hungry kitten? Or is it when I walked up to you and took your hand in mine—" his hands clenched and unclenched, as if reliving the sensations "—and it shook from the power of your response, with the promise of what it would later do to me?"

A ragged scoff escaped her. "Way to go rewriting history. I was at a loss at how to react to a stranger's forwardness."

"I was never a stranger to you. You've known who I was probably since you were old enough to know anyone."

"I knew *of* you. And what I knew accounted for the wary part of my reaction."

"What about the hungry part?" His eyes turned goading. "And I never asked—didn't Aliyah sing my praises? How… un-cousinly of her at the time, if she didn't."

"If she'd sung anything about you, I bet it wouldn't have been praises. And since you went to great lengths to divert her from your intentions concerning me, she never did the cousinly thing for *me,* and warn me to keep you at world's length."

"I diverted her in the interest of preserving the eyes you said you adored."

And those eyes, damn him, were as magnificent as ever, emitting the golden lust that put common sense on the fritz whenever he trained them on her.

"From the mother cat routine she had going with you, she would have scratched them out had she known my 'intentions.'" A frown gathered the spectacular slashes of his eyebrows. "So which first intimacy were you talking about?" Suddenly his eyes blazed with sensual challenge. "You mean when you sucker punched me?"

"I did no such thing. I gave you plenty of warning."

"*Aih,* to let you go or else. When I wasn't holding you against your will. I wasn't even touching you."

"You were backing me into a corner."

"I was walking toward you. You were the one who kept retreating, cornering yourself."

"Because you had me alone in your hotel suite."

"Where you came under your own power and of your own free will."

"I came to attend a party, with Aliyah."

"My party, in my suite. And I wasn't the one who made Aliyah leave you there to bail out one of her other lost souls."

"I was never a lost soul of hers. And I only stayed because she said she'd be back in thirty minutes."

"You still didn't leave when she was much later than that."

"I was new in New York and I thought I was safer in your suite than I would be on the streets alone at night."

"And you were."

"It didn't look like that when everyone left me alone with you. A man twice my size, twenty times as strong, not to mention a prince with diplomatic immunity and god-level entitlement."

"And you thought I sent them away to have you to myself."

"I was right."

"Not about the sinister intentions that earned me that one-two combo."

"Don't exaggerate. That follow-up punch didn't even connect."

"Only because the first one almost felled me." His hand wrapped around his throat as if feeling it again. "Not to mention the shock of the angel I couldn't wait to have turning into a harpy. *Ya Ullah,* if I wanted you one karat before that, I wanted you twenty-four then."

She'd been horrified at what she'd done, had tried to run out. He'd stopped her. Without touching her still. Just by calling to her. It had been the first time he'd called her his "silver eyes."

And just like that, her fears of who he was, of the kind of power he wielded and the unbridgeable gap that existed between them, had disappeared. He'd stopped being the son of a woman she'd grown up hating and become something far more dangerous. The personification of every forbidden desire she'd never thought she harbored. He'd been warm and accessible, witty and eloquent in ways she'd never encountered, admiring her beauty, her spunk, then teasing her about her attack, leaving her in no doubt he knew what had fueled it. Frightening attraction, which he shared in full.

He hadn't taken her to bed that night, but they both knew he could have. He'd waited two months, driving her out of her mind with wanting him in the interim. After that first time in his bed, serviced and pleasured, devoured and dominated, she'd become addicted, had wanted him with an intensity and an obsession that had sent her in a tailspin. For the next four years.

Their intimacies had been wild, greedy, explosive. But the escalating physical gratification had only plunged her deeper into emotional and psychological deprivation…

"Not that you ever need to punch me again," he said. "You knock me out just by looking at me with those spellbinding eyes, by wanting me as much as I want you." She opened her mouth to contradict him and a caressing hand below her chin closed it for her. "Don't bother. This is the one incontrovertible fact we share. So are you sure this is the intimacy you want to reenact, with so many to choose from? Like the first time we made love…."

Her assertion that they'd never "made love" went un-scoffed as he again placed a finger on her lips and the heat of his flesh almost fused them shut.

She staggered back and he sighed, dropping his hand, his eyes growing hotter as minute details of that first time replayed in their depths. "I remember every glide of skin on skin, every press of flesh into flesh, every sensation as you opened yourself to me, surrendered your every response, begged for my possession and pleasuring, as if it were encoded in my every cell. I remember each and every time after that."

She stared at him, shock and fury giving way to languor. It was as if his nearness produced chemicals inside her body that were more potent than any mind-altering drug.

No. She wasn't ever going to fall under his influence again. He'd cost her too much. And not only her...

Anxiety started to bubble and seethe inside her. She had to make sure he walked away forever this time and would avoid thinking of her for the rest of his life. But she'd been going about this all wrong.

The best way to do that was to *not* give him a challenge. Wounding his massive pride might have driven him away, had kept him there for a while, but the need to satisfy it had driven him back. She had to learn from her mistakes, if only this once.

"Memories are nice, I'm sure," she said. "But you're focusing on inconsequential memories and forgetting relevant ones. Like why you intended to delete me from your memory in the first place."

Ice suddenly extinguished the embers of sensual fire in his eyes. "I forget nothing. It's a curse Aal Shalaans suffer from. It's also why I failed to perform that deletion I intended. The moment I knew you were back here, I admitted that I never would."

She'd known about Aliyah's amazing eidetic memory but this was the first time he'd mentioned possessing something similar. But then, what had he ever *told* her? He'd *talked,* a lot, but it had all been about passion, both sexual and contentious. Besides that…nothing.

She shrugged. "This infallible memory must also mean you haven't forgotten the bad parts. And those were ugly enough to douse anything you imagine was so wonderful."

"You mean the parts where you got close to one of my best friends and conned him into marrying you, only to dispatch him in record time? Though maybe I shouldn't call 'almost two years' record time. As always, I salute your tenacity. You must have wanted to get rid of him sooner."

"So you *ass*ume."

At the reigniting challenge and enjoyment in his eyes, she almost smacked herself. *Focus. Just be a neutral bore and defuse his confrontational circuits.*

"So why don't you fix my *ass*umptions?"

She wanted to tell him to go fix himself.

Instead, she decided to deflate the misapprehension that clearly fueled his perverse interest in her.

She released her breath in a resigned exhalation. "I wasn't at liberty to disclose the matter when we…last met. I'm still not comfortable talking about it, but I guess there's no reason to keep it a secret anymore, at least from you."

"Is that your oblique way of warning me to keep this a secret? Because I'm known to be such a blabbermouth?"

"You mean you won't run to the media with my disclosures, or rush to tweet about them?" She tamped down another wave of bitterness, lips twisting with it. "But you're right. The way you keep secrets, I bet anything I tell you would be even safer than it would with a corpse. But I wasn't thinking about your ironclad discretion when you showed up two months after Patrick's death. With the turmoil I was in and the dangers I was facing, not to mention your added aggravation, sharing the truth with you was pretty low on my list of considerations."

"Are you going to share said truth now? About how he 'really' died? If it's what you told the police, don't bother."

"I don't know how the police work in this region, O Prince of Two Kingdoms, but in New York they don't care what you 'tell' them. They only listen to solid evidence. *Especially* when someone so rich and young dies of unnatural causes."

"But they found no evidence of foul play, hence my accusation a couple of years ago."

"About getting away with murder?" She cocked her head at him, hating the way her heart sputtered as his eyes followed the movement of her hair when he was more or less accusing her of being a murderess. "So you think I'm capable of it?"

"I know you're capable of driving a man to take his own life."

"Based on what? My infamous former career as a woman who used my body to make a living? Or as the woman who dared to end things with you?"

She stopped, cursing herself silently, viciously. She was sliding into inciting recriminations again.

"How about as the woman who 'used her body' to trap herself a billionaire when I didn't make the bid you were after?"

It was no use. This man could goad a rock into hurtling itself at him. "You're saying I was after a proposal? As in marriage? Did it seem to you like I thought fairy-tale movies were based on true stories? Last time I looked, those and rom-coms were the only realms where the prince married the servant's daughter."

"When you said you wanted a man who 'wouldn't hide

you like a dirty secret,' who'd 'walk with you in the sun,' you meant you wanted a proposal. You let me know I was useless to you if I didn't cough up one only when you had a suitable substitute secured."

"*Suitable substitute secured?* I bet you can't say that five times in a row." She coughed a furious laugh. "It never crossed my mind that our…liaison would be more than what it was—trivial, sporadic, not to mention base. And that's why I decided to end it. Sex was no longer enough to put up with the degradation."

"Degradation?" he hissed. "I went to every effort to make sure our…liaison, as you put it, remained only between us so you wouldn't be exposed to anything of the sort."

Bile rose again. "And I knew it couldn't have been different between us. But that doesn't mean it was okay or even sane. I was trapped in a vicious circle, wanting to end it then letting you walk back into my life anytime you pleased, to lure me back into that…toxic compulsion. *That's* why I ended it. The inequality, the unbridgeable gap, the pointlessness, on every level, was corroding my self-esteem and psychological health."

"And the only cure for both was a besotted billionaire husband."

She snorted. "That's your favorite assumption, isn't it? You have to find a mercenary, borderline criminal rationalization to explain that a woman would choose to deprive herself of you, don't you?"

"When I'm left with no explanation, apart from an ambiguous rant, I had to fill in the blanks, before and after the event."

"And you couldn't find a rationalization where you were in any way to blame, right?"

"If I were, you should have aired specific grievances and given me the chance to undo them. Instead, you chose to become hysterical before storming out. And you promptly ended any chance for me to approach you with reconciliation efforts. What could I do but adopt the harshest explanations?"

"Wow, your Cambridge English major is sure coming out to play, isn't it?"

His smile turned lethal. "So you're telling me that blowup wasn't a pretext to get me out of the picture while you grabbed the opportunity to land a far more malleable man with almost as much money?"

"Patrick was far more of a man, period, and a human being than you can ever dream of being." And she was pathetic, because knowing that had never extinguished the hunger that consumed her alive. Not that she'd let it steer her now that she had far more than herself to safeguard, to defend. "And I certainly didn't marry him for his money and assets. In fact, he married me for them."

After that first punch, Jalal had managed to anticipate Lujayn for the next two years. Her pattern had changed in the following two, but after some readjustment, he'd still charted it.

Then had come that day two years ago. Nothing had happened according to his expectations then or ever since. It was as if he'd lost his insight where she was concerned.

She kept throwing curves he remained unprepared for. She'd just insulted his manhood, his humanity. But that wasn't what he'd taken issue with. It was that riddle she'd hurled at him.

Suddenly, every frustration of the past four years blew away his intention to play this cool and seductive. The suaveness he'd maintained till now became a seething mass of urgency.

"You prefaced all this with your intention to tell me the

truth. So *b'haggej'jaheem,* skip the cryptic teasers. What in *hell* do you mean he married you for *his* money and assets?"

Those unique eyes of hers echoed his ire and passion. "Nothing cryptic to it. He wanted to make sure his wealth and projects didn't go to his so-called family after he died."

He'd demanded she give it to him straight. But he hadn't expected she would, or that much. It was so straight that his mind stalled with implications he'd never considered.

"If you were any kind of friend to Patrick, let alone one of his best friends as you like to claim, you must know his relationship with his family was…pathological, to say the least."

He nodded slowly. After Patrick's mother died, his father had married a woman who turned out to be a wicked stepmother straight out of a fairy tale. Her evil became even more evident when she had children. She did everything she could to destroy Patrick's relationship with his father to make him cut Patrick off from his inheritance. To her fury, Owen McDermott did the opposite. Unlike a typical, oblivious fictional father, he was aware of his new wife's flaws and that their children shared her hatred of Patrick. His will cut *them* off from the bulk of his fortune, leaving it to the honorable Patrick to give them what he saw fit.

And Patrick *had* given. But nothing had ever been enough.

She continued, "Patrick told me his life story the first night we met."

How he remembered that night. It had been one of the handful of times he'd gone out with her, meeting in a secluded restaurant. They'd stumbled upon Patrick who'd been out drinking alone. Jalal had been called away to handle a business emergency, and Lujayn had driven the intoxicated Patrick home. He'd thought nothing of it in his certainty of their exclusive interest in each other.

His heart clenched at the expression that came over her, as if she were looking into the past with longing and regret.

"We became friends from that night. He started coming with me on my vacations to Ireland, the homeland he hadn't returned to since his mother died. He found a new family there."

"Yours."

He didn't need her nod of corroboration. All the time they'd been together, she'd been taking another man home.

"He and my father grew very close, and along the way, Dad gave him advice that multiplied his inheritance a dozen times. His so-called family came swarming back, demanding their 'share.'"

"And he didn't want to give them any more." Her poignancy chafed him so badly he wanted to shake her out of this melancholy over another man. He clenched his fists on the urge. "So you're saying he married you to give it to you instead."

"Me and my family. We were the ones he trusted."

"Why should he have wanted to trust anyone with his fortune?"

"It wasn't simply money. He had many projects, companies and charities. He knew if his stepmother and half brother and half sisters got their hands on those, they would liquidate everything and go somewhere tropical and live like retired despots. He wanted to make sure they didn't have legal claim to any of it."

"Thanks for the elucidation, but that wasn't what I asked. Why would he prepare alternative heirs when he was so young? It's as if he knew he was going to die. Did he have psychiatric problems? Was he suicidal?"

"He certainly was not!"

Her denial barreled into him. It felt real. Too real. As if an emotional charge was building inside her as she talked about Patrick, remembered him. The mere mention of something she considered insulting to Patrick had her on the verge of another attack.

The blackness that had been roiling inside him ever since she'd left him and married Patrick spread. She'd once been passionate about her displeasure with him, but now she treated him with cold contempt. Patrick commanded her respect and allegiance, even in death. Had he been so wrong about what he'd thought they'd shared? About her relationship with Patrick?

Scowling at him as if she'd like to give him another one-two combo, she said, "Patrick was the most psychologically healthy person I've ever known. He was also the most be-nevolent. He would never have done anything to harm him-self, not only because he was stable as a rock, but because so many people depended on him."

That he knew to be true. He'd admired Patrick from the day they'd met, over fifteen years ago, for his boundless energy and enthusiasm, his progressive views, but mostly for his unswerving humanitarianism. It had been bitterness over Lujayn that had driven him to sever all ties with him, business and otherwise. That was what he'd regretted most when Patrick had died. That he had died with them at odds.

"Patrick had inoperable testicular cancer, having already spread to his major organs."

His breath clogged in his throat. He didn't know what shook him more—this revelation, or her reaction to remem-bering it.

Anguish seemed to crash over her, shaking her features, her voice. "I was with him the day he was diagnosed. He was told he had a year at most, with treatments, far less without. But he wouldn't spend what time he had left suffering from side effects when there was no chance of a cure. He wanted instead to live what remained of his life as a full member of the extended family who loved him as their own."

Something inside him withered.

He hadn't known. Hadn't even suspected. He'd been so blinded by jealousy, by his wounded pride and thwarted passion, he hadn't bothered to investigate beyond the obvious. He'd chosen to think the worst, of Patrick, and of her.

But this only exonerated Patrick. *She* might have still used his approaching mortality to entrap him.

Yet what mattered was that instead of being there for Patrick at the end of his life, he'd become his enemy.

Could she be inventing all this to exonerate herself?

He glared at her, praying he'd read something in her eyes that would tell him he hadn't been so oblivious. "You know I can unearth his medical records if I want to."

Distaste bloomed in her eyes. "That's why you have to believe me even if you hate doing so. The evil bitch you're painting me to be couldn't be stupid enough to lie about something you can so easily check."

He staggered back as more realizations pummeled him. "*Ya Ullah*...so it's true. And he hid his diagnosis so that his businesses wouldn't collapse, taking thousands of jobs with them. That's why I never heard about it."

She nodded, turned away, discreetly dabbing at her cheeks.

She didn't want him to witness her tears. He never had. He'd never driven her to them, in pleasure or pain. More proof that where he was concerned, her emotions had never been involved.

She sat down, looked at him, tears sparkling in precarious ripples. "But his doctors' predictions didn't come true. He had twenty months with us before he began to deteriorate. It was the best time of our lives. All the while he coached me and my family in what we should do once he was gone. When his decline began, it was...painful...." Tears arrowed down her cheeks. "He chose not to prolong his suffering and ours, chose to end it on his own terms."

He was breathing like he'd just escaped a runaway car by the time she fell silent. *Ya Ullah...Patrick!*

Frustration and futility crowded in his head until he felt it might burst. "How could you not tell me?"

She raised her gaze at his growl, anguish turning to incredulity. "I never gauged your ego correctly, did I? Even gods can't have that much entitlement. You see this only in terms of feeling slighted for being excluded? Why would I have told you anything, pray tell? You were no longer his friend."

"Because I didn't have a full picture. Because I didn't know what had driven him to do what he did."

"If you think his condition drove him to slam the door in your face, think again. He remained clear and calm till the hour he died. He did what he thought was right, like I did, severing a toxic relationship he realized he should have ended long ago."

"But none of his grievances against me, real or imagined, mattered. Not *then*. *B'Ellahi,* he was dying, and I should have known. *I should have been there for him.*"

She gaped at him as if he'd grown a third eye.

Figured. It was the first time she'd seen him agitated.

Then, as if trying not to rouse a beast she'd just discovered was dangerous, she said, "I would have encouraged him to tell you if I'd thought you'd feel this way. But it didn't occur to either of us that it would matter to you, beyond a passing regret for someone you used to be friendly with."

If her words hadn't paralyzed him, he would have swayed where he stood. "Is that what you both thought of me? That I am some sort of psychopath? Only one would feel nothing but 'passing regret' for such a tragedy. And I wasn't 'friendly with' Patrick. He was one of only three real friends I ever had in my life."

"I didn't know that. From observations I—" She stopped, color creeping into her blanched cheeks. "I didn't have enough observations to build an opinion on. So I filled in the blanks, like you did, with what made the most sense to me. And what most supported my analysis was that you weren't that close."

"When could I have demonstrated that closeness? I never saw him again while you were with me, as we kept our relationship a secret. But I must have let you know what he meant to me?"

Censure surged back into her gaze. "You don't remember if you did? Whatever happened to your unfailing memory? Let me boost it, then. You never did. And when he helped me make the decision to end our liaison, I assumed he knew from experience that anyone was better off not being close to you."

"Why, thanks. To both of you. It's so heartening to know you two had such high opinions of me...."

He stopped. He'd heard those words before. Or something to their effect. Haidar had communicated a similar hurt to him and Roxanne, for condemning him based on circumstantial evidence, without giving him the benefit of the doubt.

He'd lived his life thinking he and Haidar were opposites. It was becoming clearer by the day that they were truly twins. But Haidar had resolved the mess of misunderstanding with both him and Roxanne. A similar resolution wasn't in the cards for *him*.

But... "None of that explains why you kept all this a secret after Patrick died."

She gave a cheerless huff. "I had to because his family sued to annul his will. With his overdose, they were claiming what you assumed—that he wasn't of sound mind when he drew up that will. Contrary to you, who can find out anything with a phone call, police investigations and medical reports were confidential, so they couldn't know that he'd been terminally ill—which would have only strengthened their case. We had to keep it a secret until we won."

This explained so much.

The only thing it didn't explain was the way she'd walked out on him. So she'd wanted to be there for a man she'd clearly cared about, even if other factors had been involved, like his billions. There'd been no need to end things with *him* so...dramatically.

She claimed she'd suffered the "degradation," the "inequality and the pointlessness" of their relationship. Even if that had once been true, everything had changed. His situation, hers. The gap between them had almost been obliterated.

He moved, and every step closer brought her beauty into sharper focus. If he'd thought she'd filled out two years ago, now she'd ripened. And he couldn't wait to sink his teeth and...everything else into all that fire and lushness.

He held her gaze as he came to stand before her. "You should have told me, both of you. You deprived me of the chance to do what I could, what I would have wanted to do with all my heart—even if you don't think I possess one. But it's too late. The only thing I can do now is see that Patrick's legacy remains intact, that his vision for his enterprises is maintained and evolved. Will you promise to leave our... problems out of this and let me help?"

Those incredible eyes flashed again as she looked up at him, making him dizzy with desire. Then she nodded.

He exhaled, nodding, too, then sat down beside her.

"Now we need to agree on something else." Her nod was wary this time. "You have the secret code to my libido." Haidar had always said he was a wolf. And damn it, he'd turned out to be right. His body had declared her his mate, had refused substitutes. "And I have yours. When it comes to passion and pleasure, to finding absolute satisfaction in another's body, we're each other's lot."

She exhaled in resigned agreement. He held her focus, demanding she translate her consent into action. And she did. With her eyes filled with turbulent thoughts and desires, she moved into his arms as he pulled her to him, met him halfway in a kiss that made no attempt to temper its ferociousness and carnality.

Melding with Jalal's hunger and the hot vise of ecstasy that was his lips, desire swelled, flooded all considerations and obliterated every moment since she'd been in his arms like that.

She spiraled down the abyss of need as his breath mingled with hers, his hands unraveled her, his lust stoked hers, opened her recesses to his possession.

Her clothes gave way to his expert urgency, her flesh burgeoned for his dominance, her mind hazing, short-circuiting...

"From the moment you put that supple hand in mine," he groaned against her lips, "everything about you became everything I craved. Whatever happened or will happen, nothing will change that. I must have you again, and you must have me. Say yes, Lujayn. Give yourself to me again. End our starvation."

His coaxing demand went off like a warning shot in her head. The overwhelming need to obey it felt like staring into an abyss. One she wouldn't be able to crawl out of this time. Horror tore her out of her surrender to the conflagration of their mutual need.

"No."

She wrenched herself away from his body, from the desire to merge with him. She struggled up, panting. The brooding hunger that always tampered with her sanity simmered in his wolf eyes, and her heart stampeded with her internal war not to just give in, straddle him, lose her mind all over him again.

She turned, felt the world teeter with every step away from his insupportable temptation, her hands shaking uncontrollably as she rearranged her clothes.

She forced herself to turn to him at the door. "Walking away from you was the best thing I've ever done for myself and I'm not falling into your…addiction again. This isn't a challenge so you'd try harder. This is final, Jalal. I'm just putting my life back together and I won't let you destroy everything all over again. If you have any honor, stay away from me. Please."

Four

Jalal stared at the screen of his laptop.

Something wasn't right....

Frowning, he reread the document he'd just finished writing.

He was wrong. *Something* wasn't wrong. *Everything* was.

It was as if someone bent on sabotage had written the page in front of him.

But that someone was him, unable to stop obsessing over a certain ebony-haired, silver-eyed spitfire and perpetually in a state of crippling, mind-scrambling frustration.

In other words, he should be wearing a sign saying "Keep away from all rational decisions."

He closed his laptop, backed his chair from it as if it were a bomb. He *had* been about to cause an explosive mistake.

Rising to his feet, unrest fueled his strides to the veranda.

Exhaling forcefully, his eyes roamed the tranquil vastness of the desert, Lujayn's voice echoing in his head.

Stay away from me. Please.

And he had stayed away. For four weeks now.

No wonder his mind was disintegrating.

But it hadn't been honor that had made him stay away.

It had been that "please."

Had she walked out of that suite without uttering it, he would have kept going after her until she succumbed.

But—*ya Ullah.* That *please.* And that desperate look that had accompanied it. It had been their combo of pleading and dread that had depowered him, defused his intentions.

It was as if she did believe that giving in to her desires in the past had almost destroyed her life, would certainly do so now.

He couldn't see how it had, how it could. And this "degradation" thing. She'd more or less accused him of doing to her what he'd thought Haidar had done to Roxanne, manipulating and taking advantage of her.

But *their* relationship hadn't started because of a bet, as he'd thought Haidar and Roxanne's had. Haidar hadn't had an as-valid reason to hide his relationship with Roxanne, the daughter of a prominent diplomat. And Roxanne had been living in Azmahar where Haidar had almost relocated. Jalal had had to travel halfway across the world every time he'd wanted to see Lujayn.

Another major difference had been that Roxanne had told Haidar she'd loved him. Haidar hadn't reciprocated the confession, but continued their intimacies, making it appear as if he'd been taking advantage of her. There'd been no mention of anything beyond passion between him and Lujayn.

They'd been young and preoccupied with establishing their careers and *that* had enforced the sporadic nature of their relationship. The secrecy, considering what his mother would have done to Lujayn and her whole family had she suspected a thing, had been a no-brainer. What could he have done differently?

If she'd had grievances about their arrangement, she should have spoken up. She'd never done so. So he could be excused if he didn't take her unrelated temper flares at the time as evidence of past discontent. Or if he didn't accept this alleged degradation he'd exposed her to. Or her other stated reasons for walking out.

Why wouldn't she just admit she'd wanted a clean break to be with Patrick? Why was she persisting on that twisted version of history? It didn't make sense that she'd play the wronged female. It didn't sit right with her character. And she claimed she wanted one thing from him. That he stay away. Yet blame was a lure not a repellent. If she wanted him to stay away, she shouldn't have accused him and gotten him even more engaged.

Yet, he couldn't deny the authenticity of that *please*.

That left only one answer. There was more to all this than she was letting on. And to make her confess it all, he had to do one thing. Alter reality. At least, her perception of it.

He now had the means to do that. Late last night, Fadi had provided him with a windfall of a discovery. The plan to use it to fulfill all his goals had come to him fully formed.

Now before he caused actual damage—to his business, not to mention his sanity—he had to put it in motion.

He produced his cell phone. In seconds, the familiar voice rumbled in his ear like faraway thunder. *"Somow'wak?"*

He gritted his teeth at hearing Fadi calling him Your Highness. It wasn't just a title to Fadi. He meant everything it stood for. Everything Jalal felt he had no claim to.

He exhaled. "I have new orders concerning Lujayn Morgan."

A long silence stretched after he'd specified his orders. He frowned. "Fadi? Are you still there?"

"Ella, Somow'wak."

"Did you hear everything I said?"

Another long silence. A rare show of opinion from the stoic Fadi. "Are you sure about this, *Somow'wak?* These… intentions might interfere with your campaign. They might even damage it."

Of course that would be what Fadi would worry about. And if he'd voiced his concerns, he must think the consequences of Jalal's tactics could be catastrophic.

If only. If they were, it would also mean they had worked.

"You have your orders, Fadi."

This time Fadi didn't take time to answer, the matter grave enough it made him go against his unquestioning fealty. "Have you given possible ramifications enough thought? If you allow me, I can come up with an alternative scenario that would right this wrong, but keep you away from any hint of further scandal."

His lips spread as he visualized the success of *this* scenario. With Lujayn back in his bed. In his life.

"This is what I *need* to do, Fadi. And yes, I'm sure. I've never been more sure about anything in my life."

Lujayn gaped up at the dark colossus looking solemnly down at her.

Rationally, she knew he wasn't bigger than Jalal. But while Jalal made her acutely aware of her femininity, made her feel soft and pliant in comparison to his chiseled power, this guy made her feel…dwarfed, vulnerable.

Other than that, Fadi Aal Munsoori shared much with Jalal, had that force-of-nature-embodiment thing going. And like one, he'd walked into her family home and made them all feel as if they were there at *his* discretion.

Knowing everything and everyone relevant in Azmahar from her family, and everything about Jalal from her own obsessive research, she'd recognized Fadi on sight. Everyone had. He'd still introduced himself, *after* he'd walked in. It hadn't been her imagination that he'd stressed his positions as Jalal's head of security and campaign director for her benefit. And that menace had spiked when he'd specified the latter.

He hadn't been with Jalal during her time. But one look into his eyes told her he knew of their defunct relationship. And disapproved something fierce. *And* was warning her off. Had they been alone, she would have told him where he could put his precious prince and his probable future throne.

But that was before Fadi had made his offer. Something so ridiculous that her mind shrieked to a halt.

"You—you can't possibly— Prince Jalal can't possibly mean…"

The faltering words jogged her back to the fact that her mother was right beside her. Her gaze dazedly moved to her, found her looking more flabbergasted than she felt.

"*Somow'woh* says and offers only what he means," Fadi said. "I brought this information to his knowledge only last night and eight hours later he insisted I conveyed to you his gracious offer. I can understand your reluctance…"

"I-it's not reluctance!" her mother blurted out, cutting him off, to his obvious displeasure. "It's shock. I—I never thought this would ever be brought to light again."

Fadi grimly nodded. "It would have been forever buried if Prince Jalal hadn't directed me to unearth the evidence. Still, your justifiable reservations may be averted if…"

"Is it true?"

The haunted voice dragged Lujayn's gaze to her uncle. It was the first time he'd talked since he'd welcomed Fadi in. She'd totally forgotten he was there.

Her uncle had once been almost as gorgeous as Jalal, if in a very different way. His striking good looks had long been dulled, like the magnificence of a gleaming sword would be by rust.

Now something trembled below the layers of resignation, of…defeat. It was as if his soul was being reignited.

Her uncle suddenly moved, almost stumbled as he grabbed hold of Fadi's arm with a shaking hand. "Is it? Prince Jalal is in possession of proof?"

Fadi gazed at her uncle's stooped form. "He is, *ya sayyed* Bassel. At his orders, I unearthed deeply buried but incontrovertible proof. He will see to it that your family members are reinstated into *gabayel el ashraaf.*"

Lujayn knew Arabic perfectly, especially the Azmaharian colloquial dialect. She'd learned it, at her mother's insistence that language was power. So far, it had been one, in Jalal's hands. He'd used her comprehension of his verbal passion as another element of her enthrallment.

So she understood what Fadi had just said. But that couldn't be what he'd meant. When had the Al Ghamdis ever been considered among the "tribes of nobility" around here? They were from the class who emptied their ashtrays and fetched their slippers!

"Okay, time out!" Lujayn made the gesture, stepping between her mother and uncle, who vibrated with emotion, and that monolith who'd come at his master's command to spout impossibilities and spread more heartache. "What the hell are you all talking about?"

Fadi's eyes shot her a bolt of disapproval. Didn't approve of ladies swearing, eh? Tough luck. Right now, she'd do far more than swear at any further provocation.

Her uncle turned to her, that aching mixture of disbelief and hope fluctuating in suddenly expressive eyes, turning their turbid hazel into pools of agitated flame. "Our family is related to the royal family…"

"*Ex*-royal family," Fadi corrected.

The growled qualification zinged through her. Though her mind was spinning from her uncle's revelation, Fadi's vehemence still had her curious antennae standing on end. Though he was related to said family, too, those core royals seemed to have left no one with an ounce of goodwill toward them.

Which wasn't important now. She urged her uncle on with a gesture, and with her other hand she warned Fadi to just shut up and let the man explain before her head burst.

"The Al Ghamdis were once Aal Ghamdi," her uncle said, his face working as if he'd weep any moment now.

Lujayn stared at her uncle. That difference in *tashkeel*—the diacritic that changed pronunciation—transformed everything she'd ever known about her mother's *ailah*—family. It changed them from a family who took their name from a *gabeelah*—a tribe they served, to that *gabeelah* itself. It was one known for its warriors who "sheathe their swords in their enemies' chests" in the service of their kings, and second only to them.

"We are first maternal cousins to the Aal Refa'ee."

That was Jalal's mother, Sondoss's, maternal family, the other half of the royal lineage of Azmahar. The serpents named after a snake master. One quarter of Jalal's heritage.

Her gaze traveled from her uncle to her mother to Fadi. Then she burst out laughing.

At her mom's and uncle's gasps, and Fadi's deepening scowl, she spluttered, "C'mon, guys, you gotta admit…this *is* hilarious."

What could be more ridiculous than finding out that her family was related to Sondoss's? That her mother was related to her former enslaver?

That she was related to Jalal.

Another bubble of incredulity rose from her depths, burst on her lips in unrestrained cackles.

She heard her uncle's choked apologies. "I beg your pardon, Sheikh Fadi. We've never told our children, so this is a surprise to Lujayn."

"Surprise?" And she howled with laughter again, tears of hilarity beginning to pour down her cheeks, her sides starting to hurt. She leaned forward, pressing her hands to the ache clamping her midriff, barely catching enough breath to cough out words. "A surprise is when you pop up on my doorstep in New York, Uncle. This? Try identity-pulverizing cataclysm!"

Fadi pursed his lips, the timbre of his displeasure abrading. "The issue is in no way primarily your own, but your uncle's and mother's. They were the ones who lived through their family's disgrace and dispossession firsthand. And they were the ones who lived with the knowledge and injury. While you might think this rewrites *your* history and identity, it's them that this reinstatement will vindicate."

She shook her head as she straightened, his sternness suppressing the advancing hysteria. That and the sinking realization of what this meant, for the future, and for the past.

This explained so much about her mother's and uncle's characters. She'd thought they were like this as a result of their hard lives in an unforgiving land. But that thread of melancholy, of mourning, in both of them had been the result of injustice and oppression of an even worse sort than she'd imagined.

"So what happened?" She turned to her mom and uncle. "How did you get demoted from relatives to servants?"

"It's…it's a long story," her mother mumbled, looking anywhere but at her.

"Nothing can be long enough to explain this. I'm going nowhere until you tell me everything."

Before either her mom or uncle could react, Fadi raised a hand, silencing them. She was beginning to hate this guy.

"I will thank you all if you postpone your familial disclosures until I'm gone," Fadi said.

She turned on him. "You came to make your prince's offer. Now you did. So what are you waiting for?"

One dense, imperious eyebrow rose at her unveiled attempt to kick him out. Then with his voice lowering, deepening, becoming even more hair-raising for it, he only said, "An answer."

"You expect my uncle to give you an answer about something so…out of the blue, just like that?"

"What I expect him to do is talk for himself."

She'd never presumed to have a say in her family members' opportunities or decisions. But when one would involve her uncle with Jalal, she'd damn well have one. A resounding *no way!*

There was only one reason Jalal was making this offer. Her. And she'd be damned if she let him use her uncle as a bridge to reinvade her life.

She turned to her uncle, her eyes pleading with him not to commit to any answer now. His feverish eyes didn't even see her. His gaze was turned inwardly, flitting from the ordeals of his lost youth to the dream of a dignified future.

Then he turned his gaze to Fadi, his focus barely on him, either. "Please, convey my deepest gratitude to Prince Jalal for his generous offer and this unrepeatable opportunity. It would be my honor and privilege to join his campaign for the throne."

A groan bled from her as she turned her eyes to Fadi. And again his expression distracted her from her distress. Her uncle's delighted acceptance had been the last thing he'd wanted.

Sure enough, after a terse nod of acknowledgment, and a moment's thought, he said, "I was honor- and duty-bound to convey *Somow'woh*'s offer as is. But I will take the liberty of adjusting that offer, to ease the steps of your reinstatement, and to make sure no...ill-considered—" his eyes left her in no doubt this was meant for her, too "—decisions on *Somow'woh*'s part upset the delicate balance of his campaign."

If his adjustment offered her uncle anything *else* that didn't involve Jalal, she might forgive the guy. She might even kiss him for averting this catastrophe-in-the-making.

Her uncle nodded, all the animation that had been creeping into his stance and demeanor draining. "Yes, yes, of course, the first priority is to safeguard Prince Jalal's efforts."

God! What was it about Jalal that made people ready to throw themselves under a train to please him?

She knew exactly what it was. Hated him more daily for it.

"I'm offering a place on *my* team," Fadi said. "You'd still be ultimately part of *Somow'woh*'s team, as valuable to his campaign, but it would alleviate any friction that would arise from his passing over many high-ranking hopefuls for the position in your favor."

That went right over her uncle's head, lodged right into hers. Fadi thought Jalal's decision to associate with her family would be a terrible faux pas. He was trying to protect him from taking an "ill-considered" step. Not that her uncle was unqualified for the position. If anything, her uncle, who'd obtained Ph.D.s in political sciences and local and Sharia law and master's degrees in accounting and business management, was qualified to *run* the campaign. But Fadi only considered the possible damages of unfavorable public perception in a society that sequestered people into rigid classes. That "reinstatement," and the reason behind it, if it were suspected, could harm the popularity of his master and candidate. In short, Fadi was being a political weasel and privileged snob.

She still wanted to kiss him for it. His reluctance to let them contaminate his precious prince's environment gave her a way out of this new corner Jalal was backing her into.

Her uncle finally nodded. "Whatever you see fit, Sheikh Fadi. I'll be happy to offer my skills and services to Prince Jalal in whatever position I'm best suited for."

Fadi nodded, looking relieved. "I will be in touch with you shortly with further information."

He bowed respectfully to her mother, gave Lujayn a far less steep bow, clearly as deep as he thought her worthy of, then turned on his heels.

She followed him, her words for his ears only. "You think Jalal would agree to this 'adjustment' of yours?"

He slanted her a glance that seemed to measure her. No doubt wondering how his princely master had suffered being around such an unladylike creature. And was still coming back for more. "It's nothing you should concern yourself with."

"That's where you're wrong, pal. We're both on the same page on this. You don't want him near us, and I would rather he lived on another planet. So do whatever you can to 're-instate' my uncle and make use of his considerable abilities, but let's keep it all as far away from Jalal as possible. For everyone's sake."

His eyes grew incredulous. She'd managed to stun him. He probably couldn't understand how a woman wouldn't want his prince's attention. But it seemed her fervor got to him. He looked like he believed her.

For now, anyway, his gaze seemed to say. He gave her another of those military nods and strode ahead, his footsteps on the stone floor of her uncle's modest dwelling those of the soldier he'd been, and still clearly was.

He was at the door when a commotion erupted from the inner part of the house.

Lujayn froze as squeals and calls preceded running feet that came closer, intermingling with more shrieks and giggles.

Fadi stopped. Lujayn's heart almost burst.

He looked into the distance, listening, then he lowered his gaze to her. Her nerves snapped one by one in a countdown to shoving him out the door.

A split second before she gave in to the urge, he walked out.

She almost slammed the door behind him, then sagged against it, forehead first, shaking all over, scolding herself for the panic attack that had almost engulfed her reason.

Why had she been so terrified? Nothing would have happened even if he'd seen them. In a worst-case scenario if he suspected something, he would have kept it under wraps so he wouldn't sabotage his own purpose.

Not that she could grow complacent. Look what had happened when she had. Jalal had sent her a missile that was about to explode her family to smithereens.

But then…maybe the only way to dislodge said missile was with revelations of her own. She'd bet those would have Jalal taking his offer and his pursuit and running the other way.

No. Even if this was an assured outcome, she wouldn't want him to know. Not for any reason.

Exhaling heavily, she walked back to where her mom and uncle were deep in overwrought emotions, deciding she had two purposes. To shield her family from Jalal's manipulations. And to make sure that he left her and her secrets intact.

Five

Fadi's adjustments had failed in record time.

He'd called within an hour to say that Jalal's original offer wouldn't be "adjusted." Lujayn had the feeling that Jalal hadn't even let him state his suggestion.

Figured. Jalal made his decisions then made everyone bow to them. She would have wished this one would bite him in the ass, as Fadi feared it would, if it didn't involve collateral damage to more relevant parts of her family, namely their hearts and souls.

But she had a feeling Fadi had other concerns. She'd been about to probe when her uncle had swooped down on her and snatched away the phone.

She now stood watching him as he listened to Fadi. It was amazing. It was as if the man she'd known had only been animated enough to simulate the appearance of life. Now he was coming into existence for the first time under her eyes.

If she didn't hear this "long story" soon she'd bust something vital. But both her mom and uncle had so far avoided telling her anything more.

Her uncle ended the call and turned to her with a blinding and blinded expression, his voice ragged with elation. "Prince Jalal isn't only adamant about my becoming a personal adviser, but also a member of his future cabinet."

Sarcasm rose through ratcheting dismay, twisting her lips. "He's so sure he'll become king, isn't he?"

Her uncle, oblivious to her mood, gave an earnest nod. "If Azmaharians know what's best for them, they'll choose him."

"And we all know people usually steer away from what's best for them." Which to her meant they *would* go for Jalal.

Again missing her derision, her uncle said, "I believe the people will make the right choice in this instance. Prince Jalal gathers both Azmaharian and Zohaydan royal blood and the personal traits of a true leader. In short, everything Azmahar needs."

"The same could be said about his twin."

Her uncle shook his head emphatically. "Prince Haidar has stepped down from the race."

"And his new wife convinced him to step right back up."

Too engrossed in his need to prove his point, he didn't ask how she knew that. "But Prince Haidar didn't exactly rescind his decision, just qualified it by saying he'd take the throne if the majority still chose him."

"If this is a real decision and not a political maneuver, it proves he is not power hungry, yet capable of taking its mantle if it falls to him. Add that to his not spouting promises of reform if he becomes king, but being out there already deeply involved in seeing it through, and you might just have the combo that no other candidate can beat."

Her uncle's eyes took on the shrewdness of the diversely knowledgeable man he was. It never failed to stun her that, until he'd joined her in sorting through Patrick's legacy, he'd never maintained one job worthy of his skills and experience.

"Prince Haidar's efforts would have been a definite advantage," he said, "if the two other candidates weren't as involved in reforms as vital as the ones he's implementing. In fact, it's said they're all involved in the first political campaign of its kind in history."

"Sure they are. They're the first trio who're campaigning for a throne, not a presidency. I wonder why the people of Azmahar want the monarchy system to continue."

"Because before our last king, it worked too well to want to change it. Now if we pick the next, preferably Jalal in my opinion, as a king he will do far more than he'll be able to do as a president. Also you can't change the basic constitution of a people or their culture without paying a huge price, as evidenced by how badly the democracies in the region are faring. But that's not why this throne campaign is unique. It's the candidates' approach that makes it so. Instead of trying to convince people they're the better candidate by tearing the others apart, and spending untold millions to sway opinions, they're all out there showing their desire and ability to work for Azmahar's best by solving its problems now, not later. But what's really remarkable is that they're doing it together if need be. It's how they cornered the oil-spill catastrophe."

That she hadn't known. And now that she did, it stunned her.

She only knew Haidar was Jalal's twin and the male edition of their supernaturally beautiful yet soul-free mother. Evidently he wasn't as devoid of humanity as she was, since all evidence showed that he was head over heels in love with his new wife. From the grandly romantic proposal to the equally heart-fluttering wedding vows to his adoring expression in every photo with her, he actually seemed to be the reverse. She knew even less about the third candidate, Rashid, who from all reports was an unknowable quantity.

But those two men weren't only doing what all power seekers never did, putting their promises into practice first, they were curbing their egos and lust for power to do what should be done even if it meant putting their hands in their rivals'. What flabbergasted her was that Jalal was doing the same. She hadn't known he was capable of reining in either ego or lust.

"I think you've just proved that both Haidar and Rashid are as worthy, not to mention as equipped, to be king. So where do you get your conviction that Jalal is the best choice?"

"My conviction isn't built on wishful thinking as you're implying," her uncle said. "While Sheikh Rashid is a pure-blooded Azmaharian, a decorated war hero and a formidable power in the world of business, he doesn't have any ties to Zohayd. And since it's a fact Azmahar needs Zohayd to survive, let alone prosper, that's his fatal deficit. He doesn't have a chance against someone who has all of his assets plus Zohayd's king for a brother."

"That still puts Jalal in an equal position with Haidar. So unless he quits the race, Jalal's chances are only fifty-fifty."

Her uncle shook his head again. "You're assuming Prince Haidar is equal in assets, but that is far from true. He too has a fatal flaw. He bears his mother's face. You might think it shouldn't be a factor against him, but it definitely is. You of all people know how abhorred she was here."

Yeah, *that* she knew. And she'd experienced some choice abhorrent behavior firsthand.

Her uncle went on. "But Jalal doesn't suffer from this stigma. To us he's more of a Zohaydan, when Zohayd has nothing but respect, even love, for most of our population.

And he bears the likeness of his father, our biggest ally for the past decades and the one thing that had stopped Azmaharians from overthrowing our ex-king long before now. Prince Jalal is also very much like his oldest brother, King Amjad, and he'd be the one most likely to convince him to resume the vital alliance he'd severed because of the foolish transgressions of our former royalty. Added to that strong Zohaydan ingredient and influence, he has the necessary Azmaharian royal blood, making him the best of all worlds."

She gaped at her uncle, her head spinning at that unbeatable sales pitch. "Seems he did exactly the right thing in picking you for his campaign. You'd sell him to his worst enemies."

"I always believed he was the best of the candidates, always admired how he never forgot the other part of his heritage, how he'd started and supported so many worthy causes here in Azmahar long before there was any possibility of his becoming king. But now, after what he's done…" His voice thickened as he drove his hands through his silvered mane, his every facial muscle trembling with emotion. "*Ya Ullah, ya* Lujayn, you can never grasp the…the *enormity* of what he's done, the weight he's removed from my chest, what's been suffocating me all my life. If I respected and admired him before, now that I owe him my and my family's honor, now that he's renewed my will to live, I am forever in his debt."

And *that* must be exactly what that gargantuan rat was after. What better way to insinuate himself into her life than to inspire something of this intensity and permanence in her closest kin?

But she didn't believe that he'd found out about her family's secret only yesterday. As a master of manipulation, he knew how to pull people's strings as instinctively as he breathed. He must have long uncovered the secret, must have been keeping it to use when it most suited his purposes. And so he had. She'd bet her uncle, and probably her mom, too, would walk off a cliff for him now.

He'd gotten what he wanted. Just like he always did. She'd pushed him away, so he'd swerved, reentered her life from a gaping hole she hadn't known existed. She had no doubt he'd entrench himself there for as long as he saw fit.

All she could do in the meantime was thwart his intentions and steer away from him until she could flee.

Then nothing would ever bring her back.

Meanwhile, she wouldn't voice her blasphemous opinions of her uncle's newfound deity. While she believed this would end in heartache, as everything involving Jalal always did, she didn't have the guts to extinguish her uncle's rekindled appetite for life. She'd keep her apprehensions to herself. For now.

This was something her uncle and mom needed, something they hadn't let themselves dare to dream of. If they were to wake up one day to an ugly reality, she wouldn't be the one to shock them awake now. She could only speculate what Jalal's endgame would be...

"...tonight."

Her uncle's last words crashed into her train of thoughts, piling them up. He—he couldn't have said...

But, looking about to sprout wings and take flight, her uncle said it again. "You heard right. Prince Jalal has invited us all to his residence tonight to celebrate my addition to his team."

"Marhabah ya bent el amm."

The voice that had echoed in her being for most of her adult life reverberated in the still, warm night. As smooth as the steel of a burnished sword, as calm as the desert. And it had said...

Welcome, cousin.

Fury surged like a geyser. She swept around with the momentum of her frustration at being cornered again, with the blade of her family's fragile expectations held to her throat.

And she snarled, "Oh, no you don't."

In answer to her vehemence, a chuckle rumbled as if out of nowhere and everywhere, echoing on the deceptively placid breeze.

Her hairs stood on end as Jalal seemed to materialize out of the darkness, forged of its magic, imbued with its menace and magnificence. His face emerged from the velvet gloom in a masterpiece of hewn grandeur, stamped with an ancient birthright as merciless as the desert that had spawned him. His eyes reflected the flames of the brass torches flanking the cobblestone path she'd just traveled as if to the hangman's noose.

"Don't what, Lujayn? Call you what you really are to me?"

"I'm *nothing* to you."

"You were always many things to me." A smile twinkled gold in the cognac depth of his eyes, played seduction on the sculpted lips that had taught her what passion was, reminding her of every second when he'd plumbed her body and soul for ecstasies that had branded her for life. "And we discovered you're more to me than we ever thought."

"Finding out that we share a couple of stray blood cells and gene strands makes us as related as humans and apes."

"Hmm, I assume I'm the one on the lower rung of the evolutionary scale here." Merry demons licked their lips at her as he obliterated the distance between them.

"Don't." She didn't know what her "Don't" meant now. Or she did. Don't mess with her. With her will. Her need to stay angry.

"Don't what? Come closer? Like this?" She gasped as

his arm slid around her waist, and again as her body surged into his without her volition. "But you're right about my evolutionary status. Where you're concerned, at least. You devolve me to my essential beast. One who only wants to possess, plunder—" he gave a slight tug, had her melting against him from breast to thigh "—pleasure."

His feel demolished her balance and his scent deluged her lungs as her gaze flitted around frantically.

The only signs of life were the sounds of conversation and laughter emanating from the two-level sprawling villa at his back. She'd seen guards at the gates when she'd been driven into the estate's extensive grounds, but none since arriving. Maybe they were so ingeniously hidden that she couldn't even feel them.

No. He wouldn't be doing this if any eyes were around to witness it. Her driver had driven away in haste, probably following Jalal's orders for everyone to disappear once she arrived.

He'd set up his trap and lay in wait, like a panther on the hunt, now playing with her like one would torment its prey.

"Take your hands off me, or your guests will know exactly what happened to you from the way you'll limp back inside."

His grin widened, his large, talented hands securing her without force, spreading over her back in gentle caresses.

"So you'll knee me this time?" His fingers accessed the pleasure points that hadn't been activated before or since him. "I'd risk way worse to feel you like this again."

She glared up at him as every word, every gust of breath, every rub against that virility, hit her bloodstream like an aphrodisiac, spasming her core, swelling her breasts.

"And then, it's not like you don't want to feel me every bit as much." To prove his point, he took his hands away. Her traitorous body remained pressed against his.

No matter what her mind was screaming, her every inch was begging for his feel, for everything. And it made her furious. Far more with herself than with him. For he was only making her admit and succumb to her weakness. She was the one responsible for it.

Yet when she spoke, she seethed, "So you had your fun forcing me to come here and to endure your pawing without being able to retaliate. Can I go now?"

The teasing in his eyes intensified. And that pout. She didn't know how she kept from grabbing him by that mane that brushed his collar and yanking down his head so she could bite him. "First, you're here of your own free will, as usual, as my esteemed guest and newfound if admittedly distant cousin. Second, you can retaliate in any way you choose. I'll wear the marks of your passion with pride. Third…" He gathered her closer again when she didn't step away, let her feel his daunting hardness throb into her belly. "I haven't had my fun yet, not by a long shot."

She barely held back from grinding into him. "You should have one of your concubines take care of this…big problem."

Another chuckle revved in his expansive chest. "It's you who made it that big when you didn't show up with your family."

Her uncle and mom had been puzzled and dismayed when she'd excused herself from going. But she hadn't been able to come up with a good enough reason why. She'd thought even the *real* reason wouldn't have been good enough for them.

So she'd pretended to cooperate but when the escort team Jalal sent had arrived, she'd said she'd gotten distracted, wasn't ready and they'd had to go without her.

She'd thought she was saved, for that night, at least. Then the call had come. Her mom was distraught, thought her absence had offended Jalal. Why else would he so closely inquire why she hadn't come? Knowing she had to capitulate,

Lujayn had promised to be ready this time when he sent a limo for her. And here she was.

"Excuse me for not prioritizing your whims," she gritted out, careful not to breathe deep or be flooded with his intoxication. "It wasn't high on my list to drop everything to 'celebrate' my uncle being roped into your servitude for life."

His smile was all forbearance. "Had you been here the past three hours, you would have heard your uncle and mother expressing how happy they are to finally claim our relation and how excited about our forthcoming collaboration."

"That's what you're calling this artificial situation you've manufactured?"

"I didn't create this gem of a 'situation.' I'm only making the best use of it after uncovering it."

"Uncovering any tie between us, no matter how insignificant and distant isn't a gem, it's a…a…*semm*."

And there it was. That pout, again. "Poison? Aren't you getting this backward? It was the dishonor your family unjustly suffered that's been poisoning their lives. And it is that grudge you're nursing against me that's been poisoning yours."

"And you're the benefactor who wants to administer the antidote out of the goodness of your nonexistent heart? My family is free to be eternally grateful for your crumbs of benevolence, and I'm free to prefer my poison, which is at least gulped down with no strings attached."

"Take a deep breath, Lujayn." He smiled down at her as he bent, had his lips tracing her every feature with feather-soft torment from her forehead to her lips to her pulse point. "Go to your happy place for a moment."

Electricity forked from his lips to shriek down her nerves. The blow of arousal finally had her lurching out of his loose hold, had her glaring her resentment up at him. "Can't do that. You've left me none."

Lightness deserted his eyes and stance by degrees, until he stood brooding down at her. "I won't even touch that exaggeration, Lujayn. But whatever our problems in the past were, this is me taking the steps to eliminate them."

"What—what do you mean by that?"

He shoved his hands into his pockets, his eyes growing serious. "In our last confrontation, you mentioned the 'unbridgeable gap' between us. It made me realize that while I never thought there was any real gap between us, you did. This gap, whether real or imagined, is no more."

She gaped at him. Did he mean…?

Then she snorted. "If you mean it was all in my mind, please! Anyone with half a brain lobe would say the gap was actually a gulf. And that it will always remain unbridgeable."

"Not true. While it never meant a thing to me, that so-called gulf that existed between us on a social level, with the new discoveries of your true lineage, it no longer exists."

"Wow, really? You're saying some second-grade royal blood equals being from a line of purebred kings and queens and the son of one of the most venerated kings in the region, the *world*?"

His shoulders rose and fell in a dismissing move. "I also come from the line of an ousted king and I am also the son of the most infamous ex-queen in that same world. You fare better in any comparison coming from a lineage of hardworking, honest people on one side and another unanimously known for valor and honor."

"You mean that side of my lineage that was stripped of honor and reduced to serving their so-called relatives?"

He exhaled. "That's in the past now. Your line will be

restored. When everything's out in the open, they will be looked upon with greater sympathy and respect than ever."

"And this will happen only according to your whim."

"According to the proof Fadi uncovered."

"I meant you used this proof because you saw fit to. It could have remained buried for all you cared if it wasn't to your advantage to make it public now."

"The timing is fortunate, I can't deny that." That smile, fueling his irresistibility, was back radiating from his eyes, filling his lips. "Are you suggesting I shouldn't have brought it out in the open because I stand to gain from doing so?"

He had an answer for everything, could twist anything to make himself come out looking right, logical, honorable even.

"You're unbelievable, you know that? You're in the middle of campaigning for a throne, and you waste time going to all this effort to get into my pants? You're taking asserting your will and winning this imaginary challenge too far, aren't you?"

He shrugged again, that movement laden with lazy poise. "Apart the fact that I *would* do anything to 'get into your pants,' I would have done this for anyone."

"Yeah, sure, you go around investigating people to see what wrongs were dealt them in generations past so you can right them."

His nod was infuriatingly calm. "I do what I can when it comes to my notice, yes."

"Well, you might as well take back anything you've done for my uncle and family now and not later."

His eyebrows rose in feigned questioning. "You think I'll do that after I have my way with you…again?"

"After you make sure you're not having it, ever again."

His tut-tut was indulgence itself as he gently pulled her against his will-sapping gorgeousness. "Is this a way to talk to a newly discovered distant relation?" Her neck arched for him as he nuzzled it, her body plastering to his as his hands dipped below her blouse to spread against the burning skin of her back. He suddenly groaned against her flesh, which vibrated with need. "Sooner or later, you won't be able to resist me, won't find a reason to. I've already given up trying. This…affinity we share is unstoppable, *ya jameelati'l feddeyah.*"

That sick jolt of longing lurched inside her heart. He'd always been too generous with his verbal passion. Hearing him call her his silver beauty brought a wave of moisture to her eyes that intensified the illumination of the full moon. She turned her face away from its glare and his lips trailed a path of fiery temptation down her cheek, her jaw.

A shudder shook her when he reached her ear, his croon pouring into her brain, liquefying it. "We're going to be together in many ways from now on. Through my involvement in Patrick's legacy, through your family's involvement with me. This—" he crushed her against him, giving her aching breasts the contact they needed with his hardness and heat "—is inescapable."

Wariness, logic, hostility were disintegrating, everything else inside her yearning to expose his flesh, to sink her teeth in his power. Everything else was receding, leaving only the need to drag him on top of her on the lush lawn, open her body to his invasion, writhe beneath him as he thrust her to ecstasy.…

"You might as well stop fighting the inevitable now."

Suddenly, she snapped out of spiraling down the abyss of lust and pushed against him, arms feeling like a rag doll's.

He let her push him, showing her he'd only been holding her with her own desire.

Her palm spread against the vital wall of his chest. "So

what's this inevitable thing? Another affair? While I'm here?"

He took the hand splayed against his chest to his lips, singed its clammy flesh with nibbles. His eyes blazed with the passion that had once made her feel craved to her last cell. "It's another affair for as long as we both want. If you leave, I'll forever come to you, like I always used to."

"And this social-status upgrade and cleansing you gave my family, and therefore me, is so we wouldn't sully your image if our liaison is discovered?"

"Of course not."

In spite of herself, his earnestness thrilled her. Could it be he didn't care about her status, now or before...?

He aborted all foolish conjectures. "You have my word our relationship would not be discovered. My efforts were for your family, and for you, so you would no longer feel any inequality in our situation."

So. No matter who or what she was or became, he'd always think her only good enough for an illicit liaison.

He'd polished her family name, not because he cared, or even intended to ever let her name be linked to his, but to placate her. To give her a false sense of worth. To make her feel good enough about herself so she'd walk back into his bed without the insecurities that had plagued her in the past.

Something she'd sworn she'd never feel again, corrosive oppression and shame, spread to eat through her vitals.

No. She wouldn't let him do this to her again. She'd promised Patrick she wouldn't.

She tugged her hand away from his. His arms fell to his sides, didn't try to pull her back.

He still attempted to with words. "Don't push me away, Lujayn. The past is done, and I don't want to bring it up again. We're here and now, and everything is different."

She smoothed trembling fingers over her hair and clothes

that the tiny taste of his passion had messed, stepped farther away.

"That's where you're wrong, *Somow'wak*. Nothing's changed. Or if it has, it's for the worse. Sex without emotions or the most basic commonalities would only end up in something catastrophic this time."

He balled his fists as if against the urge to grab her. "Who says there aren't emotions? And we do have commonalities. Starting with how much we crave the hell out of each other and ending with our common interest in upholding Patrick's legacy and seeing to your family's reinstatement."

"And we can each take care of all cravings and interests without the other's participation. It's even advisable, just ask your campaign manager. So why don't you go pour all that drive into becoming king? You have my uncle chomping at the bit to help you sit on that throne. Contrary to me, he believes in you. Me, I'm here only until Aunt is well enough and she's almost…"

He frowned. "Your aunt?"

"Your investigations didn't bother to uncover more about me and my family than what would have us in your debt, right?"

"What's wrong with Suffeyah?"

She blinked, surprised by his apparent concern, that he not only knew but remembered her aunt's name.

He made an impatient, prompting gesture. Warily, hesitantly, she told him, watching him closely, trying to analyze the solemn intensity in his eyes as he listened.

"…the specialists agreed she only needed a simple mastectomy, which she had two weeks ago. We're now waiting to see if they'll forgo chemo and radiation and have her just on antihormonal treatments. Test results so far support that, so we're looking at a few weeks at most before everything is concluded. By that time you'll probably be the new king of a country where I never intend to return for the rest of my life."

He said nothing after she stopped talking, just brooded down at her. Might as well take advantage of the temporary interruption in his temptation campaign.

She moved away on unsteady legs, adding over her shoulder, "I'll attend what's left of your 'celebration,' for my family's sake. If you don't intend to reconsider your intentions about that 'reinstatement' and Uncle's position now that you know mine, you'll be civil and impersonal with me for the rest of this infernal night. Then I'll leave and you won't come after me again."

He folded his arms over his chest. "I thought you had a reason for pushing me away. Now I'm certain you do. There's something more behind your refusal to be with me again. And I *will* keep coming after you until you tell me what it is. I will…"

"*Somow'wak.*"

The quietness of the word sundered the still night. *Fadi*.

As much as she hated thinking that Fadi had witnessed Jalal's near-seduction of her, his appearance had shattered Jalal's focus. Cursing something under his breath, Jalal turned to him.

Using his distraction, she strode to the marble steps that glowed with the moon's silvery light. They led to a vast veranda where open French doors emanated golden light, mellow music and relaxed merriment.

As she crossed the portico, she looked back at Jalal and Fadi. The two juggernauts were watching her, each with a different brand of intensity that invaded her taxed nervous system with a fresh bout of tremors.

Suppressing her agitation, and taking one last bracing breath, she stepped over the threshold of a superbly decorated sitting room drenched in soothing illumination and spread in warm earth colors, feeling she was stepping onto a stage.

She forced a smile as everyone rose to welcome her, and started playing the part that Jalal had cornered her into again.

Jalal watched Lujayn disappear inside the villa, heard voices rise in welcome. Gritting his teeth, he turned his eyes to Fadi.

Before he could pour some of his frustration and displeasure over him, Fadi preempted him.

"I might regret telling you this, but you need to know."

This was about Lujayn. He just knew it was.

If it was something that might drive her further away, he didn't want to know it.

But Fadi was already talking. Already telling him. And it was too late. Too incomprehensible. Too…impossible.

Long after Fadi had delivered his report, Jalal stared at him, nothing left in his mind, in the world, but five of the words Fadi had said.

"Lujayn Morgan has a child."

Six

Jalal walked into the room he'd left half an hour ago to intercept Lujayn. He'd thought he'd walk back in alongside her, with at least a preliminary agreement to resume their intimacies.

He returned alone now to find her looking relaxed and at home with her family, the center of his guests' attention. At his entry, as the others showed their pleasure and enthusiasm to have him back, she regarded him as if she'd never seen him before.

He looked at her in the same way. He did feel as if he was looking at a stranger. A breathtaking stranger with crystal cool eyes who lived inside the body of the woman who'd ruled his thoughts and desires for too long. The woman he'd thought he'd known to the last reaches of intimacy but whom he was finding out that he'd never known. The woman who hadn't even hinted at the life-changing fact of being a mother.

This had to be the answer he'd been looking for—why she'd been adamant about pushing him away. Because her life and priorities had changed, *she* had changed, when she'd had a child.

The knowledge rocked through him all over again as he watched everyone returning to their seats, all looking at him expectantly, waiting for him to direct what remained of this gathering.

He looked from Bassel and Faizah, Lujayn's uncle and his wife—people he'd met for the first time—to Badreyah, her mother. He'd decided getting close to Lujayn would be through those who constituted the major part of her life. He'd been determined that, even if he found nothing about them to like, he'd put up with them. He would have endured anything to have her again.

To his surprise and delight, they'd stopped being a means to an end within minutes of meeting them. Everything about and from them had felt genuine, heartfelt. It had restored his jaded senses to be shown esteem without fawning, gratitude without groveling. They were good-natured, highly educated, well-spoken. They were dignified, refined. The hours he'd spent in their company had been a pleasure he'd looked forward to repeating on a regular basis.

Until Fadi had detonated that revelation.

Not that he would renege on restoring their name and honor. Or the position he'd offered her uncle, for which he was more than qualified. But any further personal interaction depended on what he found out about Lujayn's child.

He hadn't even asked Fadi if her child was a girl or a boy.

He hadn't asked how old it was. *Whose* it was.

Even if Fadi knew the answers, Jalal hadn't wanted to know them. Not from him. Lujayn had to be the one who answered his questions.

And he wanted those answers now. *Now.*

His head and heart felt they'd rupture with the frustration of not knowing. But no matter how terrible the need to know was, he had to proclaim his commitment to the Al Ghamdis first.

Forcing a smile on his spastic lips, he looked over to Labeeb, his *waseef,* his gentleman's gentleman. Taking his role as seriously as Fadi did his, Labeeb was already enacting the agreed-on sequence, distributing coffee, the stage where Jalal would deliver the evening's summation and declare his intentions.

After everyone had filled crystal cups in hand, and the aroma of freshly brewed Arabian coffee and cardamom filled the air, Jalal moved to face the gathering. Apart from the quartet of Lujayn's family, there were fourteen other people: four men and three women—the supporting players in his campaign—plus their spouses.

He enveloped them in a glance, avoiding looking at Lujayn. If he looked at her now, he'd forget everything.

He raised his glass in a toast, waited until everyone did the same, then said, "Thank you for coming to my humble rented abode, and for making this evening far better than anything I could have anticipated. You know what we're celebrating tonight, but let me make it official." He turned his eyes to Bassel, found him flushed, eyes sparkling with barely repressed emotion. "It's my privilege and pleasure to welcome Sheikh Bassel Aal Ghamdi to our campaign. Sheikh Bassel has honored me by accepting the position of my personal liaison within our campaign. He'll be coordinating your efforts and reporting directly to me or to Fadi."

Murmurs of approval buzzed throughout the room as everyone turned to Bassel shaking his hand, patting him on the back and congratulating his family. Bassel and his wife and sister looked too moved to articulate, could only answer with tearful smiles. Jalal ventured a look at Lujayn, found her accepting collateral congratulations. He bet it was only he who could see that her smile was brittle and her eyes were cold with fury. He walked closer, until she raised grudging eyes to his.

His heart thudded at their inevitable effect as he insisted her family remained seated as he shook their hands again, sealing the deal. "And though Sheikh Bassel was reluctant to flaunt the scope of his expertise, no matter how much I prodded him throughout dinner, trust me when I say we've added an invaluable asset to our team today. I'm only thankful for the circumstances that brought his abilities to my attention."

Ire sparked in Lujayn's eyes. She clearly didn't appreciate those "circumstances."

He swerved his focus to the others. "Now with Sheikh Bassel's contribution, if I don't get that throne, you'll know you've just bet on the wrong horse."

Laughter rose. He had to conclude this before the general good mood snapped the tenuous control he had over his increasingly agitated one. He hated to bring up the touchy subject, but he needed his aides to be absolutely clear about it.

His gesture indicated he had more to say. Instant silence fell as every eye turned to him again.

"But I didn't only gain an instrumental supporter and adviser today but a valued relative, one who's totally on my side. *Ullah beye'ruff*—God knows I don't have many of those right now, and I need all I can get." Chuckles were leashed this time, realizing this was no laughing matter even if he made light of it. His lips twisted in concession. "Which brings me to the most important issue at hand. You all now know how Sheikh Bassel and his family have been unjustly stripped of their name and status...."

"Actually, we don't *all* know. *I* sure don't."

Lujayn. Leave it to her to break her silence only to say

something contentious. From the gasps that issued from her family, it appeared her forwardness had distressed them. They evidently thought she might offend him. If only they knew how hard she'd tried and failed to do so.

He turned his eyes to her, turmoil seething with challenge. "You mean no one shared the details with you?"

Her eyes raised his annoyance. "Apart from 'long story'? No."

"And this is not the time to recount it." Bassel put a hand on his niece's, a gesture imploring her to leave it.

She didn't. "When is a better time than now, with all relevant parties present, so this new beginning would be built on a solid ground of full disclosure?"

At this moment he wanted to roar for everyone to get out, leave him alone with her so he'd have that full disclosure. Whether it led to a new beginning or a final end, he had no idea.

"Prince Jalal, please excuse Lujayn," Badreyah said, a tremor traversing her soft voice. "This has been quite a shock for her, to find out we've hidden something of this nature all her life…."

He raised his hand, unable to bear having this gentle lady apologize to him when he would never be able to offer enough amends. "No need to explain, *ya* Sheikha Badreyah."

The woman lurched, those near-tears filling her eyes again.

Jalel could see that she'd accepted her brother would have his sheikh title once again, but hadn't expected to hear the title applied to herself. But that was what she was, and that was what he'd always call her.

"Wow, does this make *me* a sheikha, too?"

Lujayn again. Lujayn *always*.

"If it does, I'm giving you all license to *never* call me that."

No longer pretending that anyone else had his attention, he approached her. "So what will you answer to?"

Those silver eyes narrowed, their ebony lashes that he'd once told her were thick enough for him to lie down on intensifying the light they seemed to emit. "My name has been known to work just fine."

He almost touched her legs as she sat on the couch, could see himself going down between them, dragging them over his shoulders, bearing down on her to crush those rose-petal lips and swallow those contentious words. He could feel everyone's eyes clinging to them, no doubt sensing the field of tension they generated between them now that they were no longer harnessing their emotions.

"So...*Lujayn.*" He stressed each syllable as if tasting it, felt a rev of satisfaction as her pupils fluctuated, that sure sign of response. "In the name of full disclosure, let me tell you the whole story. This mess happened in the time of your grandfather. And my grandmother."

Her eyes widened. "You mean your grandmother was involved?"

"Involved?" He gave a bitter huff. "You could say that. She was the one who accused your grandfather of a very potent mixture of theft and treason. But never fear. She was merciful in her righteousness and when he was convicted, she asked for a compassionate demotion in lieu of banishment or imprisonment. When your uncle was fifteen and your mother was twelve, their family lost a tiny bit of their name, becoming Al—instead of Aal—Ghamdi, and stumbled from a high branch of nobility into dishonor. Your grandfather had been my grandfather's *kabeer'l yaweraan*—head of the royal guard, but after his conviction, neither he nor any of his family could find a position in the kingdom. Again, only my grandmother was humane enough to employ them, as her servants. Also as per her clemency, your grandfather's transgression along with his family history was to never be talked of again. At the threat of some very creative penalties. It was, of course, so your family wouldn't relive the disgrace, being reminded of what they lost. Needless to say, no one, starting with your family, brought it up again ever since, and the whole debacle has been suppressed or forgotten."

Silence rang in the wake of his searingly blunt account.

Lujayn gaped up at him, the shock reverberating inside her buffeting him in waves of furious incredulity.

Suddenly, she heaved up, almost sliding against his body on her way to her feet, sending awareness roaring inside him in spite of everything.

She glared at him, antipathy crackling silver bolts in her eyes. "I should have known your family had something to do with this. But they had *everything* to do with it. Your mother fell right off *her* mother's tree, didn't she?"

"Lujayn! Stop it!"

Her mother's mortification barely registered on Jalal's inflamed senses. All he felt was this mass of incendiary passion seething at him. He was a hairbreadth from forgetting everyone surrounding him, and the questions eating at him.

"Your grandmother framed my grandfather, didn't she? Over something personal, right? And with the only evidence being her word? You discovered his innocence easily enough, after all, when you bothered to scratch the loose dirt she buried my family under, right?"

His jaw muscles bunched. "That just about sums it up."

She snorted. Gasps rang from around the room this time.

"So why didn't the truth come out after she was dead? Because your mother picked up the torch after her? And why not when *she* was exiled? Then when your uncle and cousins were ousted? Why did everyone remain silent including my martyred family? Why did it take your so-called accidental digging for some other irrelevant purpose to uncover this piece of gratuitously evil art?"

"*B'Ellahi,* Lujayn, what's gotten into you?"

Lujayn tossed her distraught uncle a glare before swinging her gaze back to Jalal, slamming him with the force of her outrage. "Do you think I'm crossing a line here, Your Highness? You think I shouldn't be angry for a few minutes for the decades of my family's disgrace and oppression at the hands of yours?"

Bassel surged, caught her arm, agitation blasting off him. "Lujayn, you *are* way over the line here."

Badreyah placed a trembling hand on Lujayn's other arm. "Whatever happened between our family members in the past has nothing to do with Prince Jalal or his mother."

Lujayn rounded on her, her scowl spectacular, her voice a magnificent snarl, one worthy of a lioness. "Really? You mean she had to show you her compassion and employ you, of all people, as her head slave and punching bag? She had to deprive you of continuing your education at only fourteen so you can fetch her slippers and be the lab rat on which she perfected her cruelties? Excuse me as I *don't think so.*"

Jalal's heart twisted with the force of shame. He felt sullied by yet another permanent taint inflicted by his family and his mother. By guilt for never bothering to find out Lujayn's real history, or the extent of the abuse of her mother by his.

"It's in the past," Badreyah insisted. "And the moment Prince Jalal found out the truth, he not only took the necessary steps to reinstate our family, he offered your uncle a prestigious position he offers only to those he considers most trustworthy."

"So we're supposed to bend backward and yodel his praises?" Lujayn growled. "Then prostrate ourselves forehead-first in thanks? Or do we even need to go further and…"

"Lujayn!"

Her uncle's soft admonishment finally brought her tirade to a halt, though she still vibrated with affront and anger.

Any other time, an hour ago, before he'd found out about her child, he would have reveled in the sheer magnificence of her fury and antagonism. He would have only invited her to hit him with more, vent all the justified ferociousness of her rage.

But he'd expended the last vestiges of his restraint. He had to end this, *now.*

He moved away from her, stood facing the others who looked like they'd rather the ground split and swallowed them.

Unable to agree more with the sentiment, he drew in a deep inhalation, unlocked his jaw. "Thanks everyone for coming and helping me celebrate Sheikh Bassel joining our team. We'll have another meeting soon to discuss our future structure and strategies in depth. But I think we're all ready to end this evening now."

He thought he heard Lujayn mutter, "Boy, am I," could almost hear the collective sigh of relief that issued from the group, venting their rising tension.

His lips twisted wryly. "Yes, everyone, if you're waiting for me to spell it out, you *can* go."

Lujayn was the first one to move, not sparing anyone another look, as if it would be too soon if she never saw anyone present again, maybe even including her family.

Everyone else gave him uneasy smiles and handshakes, relieved to escape the embarrassing situation. Her family seemed mortified and sounded like they'd never regretted anything as much as insisting that she come.

He stopped their attempted apologies, assuring them that ending the evening was for their sake not his. Look-

ing marginally reassured and even more grateful, they followed Lujayn.

As everyone cleared the doors, he called out after them,
"I said everyone can go. But 'everyone' does not include
Lujayn."

Lujayn shook under wave after wave of outrage.

She would have marched out and handed Jalal his head
if he'd tried to stop her. Too bad it had been her family who
had, with nothing but the force of their mortification. Even
as fury disabled her brakes, her innate desire to please them
had won. *Jalal* had won. He'd known exactly what buttons
to push to get what he wanted from her.

Now he closed the doors after the last departing guest.

"What's this? Detention?" she seethed as he turned to
her. "For talking back to the headmaster? You did have us
sitting there like kids who had to placate you or risk failing.
Worse, like hostages forced to put up with the theatrics of
our captor in fear of our lives."

He stopped steps away, his eyes like turbid honey, something unsettled and unsettling buzzing. "I didn't see you
placating me or putting up with anything."

A frisson of danger skewered through her.

Which was ridiculous because she'd never feared him.
But his inexplicable intensity had her heart quivering. And
it made her even angrier. If he thought he could intimidate
her into cowering or simpering like he did all the others, as
someone who didn't give two figs about his rank, wealth
and power, she was obliged to adjust his inflated view of
his importance.

"You got enough of that from the others to turn the stron-
gest stomach," she hissed. "Not to mention the truckloads
of adulation you got from my family. I always knew your
family screwed mine over in so many ways, but to find out

the real depth of their abuse, their...*crimes,* and to have the sordid details accompanied by my family's gratitude and martyrdom was just too much. So if you detained me to chastise me for daring to voice my disgust in front of the thralls you call your campaign managers, let me tell you I'm only sorry that I didn't get to say more before my family's grossly misplaced sense of decorum and their impending collective stroke silenced me."

The ferocity in his gaze rose with her every word. It made her barrel on. "Here, let me tell you what I would have said. I would have moved from condemning your family to condemning you directly. Your family members were straightforward in their subjugation of mine, showed them the kindness of open cruelty, leaving them the dignity of knowing their enemy and the relief of being able to hate them in their hearts. But your pretense of compassion and generosity is far worse since it makes them unaware of your abuse, and tricks them into being your slaves by choice."

His stare remained unwavering, as if he were trying to read her mind, to decipher her last thought and impulse. But why, when she was whacking him over the head with it all?

Maybe she needed to be even more explicit. "You must think you've succeeded in using them to have me where you want me, since they almost pleaded for me to stay when you ordered me to. So enjoy this triumph because it'll never be repeated. From now on, they know to leave me out of any feet-kissing rituals. And if you're thinking of new ways to pressure me, let me tell you now nothing else will work. This Prince of Two Kingdoms thing clearly works on Azmaharians programmed to bow down to their royalty. But even if I wasn't now a businesswoman who's long left behind any tendencies to be bowled over by you, I'm an American and we generally have allergic reactions to royal entitlement."

"Is that all you are, Lujayn?"

She blinked. His voice. She'd never heard it like that. Like the roll of approaching thunder. And what did he mean…?

"A businesswoman, an American. Aren't you leaving something vital out?"

She frowned at that searing spike of emotion in his eyes, her heart starting to thud with confusion and wariness. "If you're talking about my Azmaharian side, think I might have royalty-worshipping tendencies to unearth, save it. My only local ingredients are some genes and a passport that I never use."

Suddenly he was closer, and not because he'd moved. It felt as if he'd expanded, as if everything inside him had reached out to engulf her. She felt him all over her, inside her head.

Then in that heart-snatching tone, he said, "I'm talking about your maternal side. I'm talking about the ingredients that make you a mother."

Jalal had no idea what it was.

Maybe it was the stiffness that invaded her body, or the pulse going haywire in her throat, or the blast of horror in her eyes. Or it was all of that and myriad other instantaneous, involuntary signs that coalesced and painted a picture worth a thousand confessions.

It all added up to one thing. One thing that lodged in his mind with the force of an ax. Something devastating. The truth.

Lujayn's child was his.

Seven

The knowledge mushroomed in Jalal's skull.

Lujayn had had his child.

He had a child.

"Jalal…"

Numb to his recesses, paralyzed in soul before body, he stared at her stricken eyes, his ears ringing with the softness of the dread in her voice. His heart, his mind, everything he was made of, swelled with the enormity of the belief, unraveled with the scope of its implications.

Moments ago he'd been just himself, the man he'd been struggling to formulate a peace treaty with all his life. And she'd just been herself. The one woman he wanted, and with whom peace seemed an ever-receding mirage.

Now he no longer knew who either of them were.

They were no longer the once-lovers who sparred and parried with nothing but consuming passion at stake between them. They were two people who shared far more than their unquenchable, if according to her, better-off-suppressed needs.

They shared a *life*. They had since she'd conceived his child. But by hiding the fact, she'd stopped it from becoming a reality to him. It had only become one the moment he'd known of it.

The instant freeze that had struck him, buried him under layers of icy shock, started to crack under the heat of her dismay. Then she relinquished his gaze, swung around. The curtain of raven gloss cascading down her back arced with the force of the motion, lashed his cheek. Then she was receding like a wobbly image from a dream.

He found himself launching after her, his need to stop her, to demand…everything, propelling him.

He caught her at the door, his fingers digging in her flesh through her long-sleeved jacket, felt like they'd sunk into lava. She twisted in his hold and he brought both arms crossing beneath her heavy breasts, felt as if he'd enfolded a live wire as he subdued her against his vibrating body.

"No more fighting me off, Lujayn." Was that his voice? That wounded beast's? "I'm never going to let you walk away from me again." He turned her around, not knowing if it was his hands that were shaking or the shoulders he held her by, or both. "This is no longer a game."

She tried to shake off his hands, her eyes escaping his. "Thanks for admitting it was a game all along. But you're right. It's not, because I'm not playing. Game over, Jalal."

He almost ground his teeth to powder as the last vestiges of shock melted in the blast of rising rage. "It was you who've played me all along. *You never told me you had my child.*"

Her gaze met his at his shout, attempted derision, but the dread she'd managed to leash blossomed again, betraying her. "Don't be ridiculous.…"

"No, you don't." He gave her back her earlier fury. "Don't you *dare* try to misdirect me again. It won't work. Not only did you have my child and didn't tell me, you were *never* going to tell me."

The acknowledgment in her eyes incinerated any wisps of uncertainty into nothingness.

And he realized. That he'd hoped. For some indication that she'd hesitated in that decision. That it had weighed on her. That she'd afforded him a trace of consideration before ruling him out.

She hadn't.

He let go of her shoulders, stumbled back under the cruelty of realization, his eyes burning as they searched hers. "*Ya Ullah, ya Lujayn...b'Ellahi...laish?* Why?"

Her eyes wavered. The vulnerability of consternation gave way to the toughness of control again.

"You're kidding, right?" she scoffed. "The question is, why should I have told you?"

She truly didn't see why. How could this be? "You didn't think I should know I've fathered a child?"

Her stiff shoulders jerked. "You've probably fathered a dozen children you don't know or care about. What's one more?"

His hand rose to his chest, almost convinced he'd encounter something sharp sticking out of it. "Is this what you think? That I'm not only indiscriminately promiscuous, but that I go around having unsafe sex?"

"Seeing as how safe sex wasn't one of your considerations with me, why should I think other women warranted any better?"

He'd only ever had "unsafe" sex with her. She'd been a virgin and he'd unfailingly observed safety before her. He'd only protected her from pregnancy at first then she'd done so later. He'd thought employing contraceptive measures herself had meant she'd wanted to enjoy full intimacy, something he'd never considered doing before her. What he'd gotten addicted to with her.

And she'd thought he was... "...so callous I care nothing about the consequences, to the women I bed, and to children I must occasionally sire?"

"So you 'care'? And engage in that delightful practice you royalty types favor in this region, giving your illicit spawn the coveted title of *mansoob*? So generous of you to 'occasionally,' 'sort of' proclaim responsibility for your offspring from unsuitable wombs. The children of your servants or anyone inferior to you must be so grateful to be declared illegitimate but 'associated' with you. So isn't it just lucky for me that I don't need your 'association'? And neither does Adam."

Adam. His child was a boy. And he was nineteen months old.

The extent of what he'd missed in that time felt like a noose tightening against his windpipe, suffocating him. And for the first time in his life he knew what it meant to be helpless.

This chunk of his child's life was gone, and he could never get it back, for either of them.

It must have showed on his face, the anguish and defeat. It twisted her stony expression into a grimace.

"Let's not pretend this was something you considered at all, let alone with me. You didn't even acknowledge me, but you would have my baby? But it wasn't your fault I got pregnant. You probably thought I was protected. I wasn't. I let contraception go when I married Patrick."

So if it had been her choice, her child would have been her husband's. She'd had his only by mistake.

"Then he died, and sex was the last thing on my mind, so when you popped up out of nowhere and we ended up in bed, repercussions didn't even occur to me except when my period was a month late. So it's really none of your business that I got pregnant. Adam is none of your business, just like I never was."

Bitterness choked him. "You were never my business? I was unable to have a moment, waking or sleeping, for eight years without thinking of you, craving you...*obsessing* about you."

"Lighten up on the exaggerations, please," she sneered. "I was there, remember? At least through the years we had together. I know for a fact that during those, you spent weeks, sometimes months, without doing any of that."

"I never stayed away by choice, and all the time we were apart, I did *all* that. Then you left me, and the moment I thought it possible to come to you again, I did."

Her eyes flared silver fire. "And you came to have closure or sex or both, not father a child."

"I told myself I came for the first. But what I really wanted was to clear away the bitterness, at least come to terms with it so I can...reconnect with you, claim you again."

"You never connected with me or claimed me to start with."

"That's your version. Or maybe it was the truth, for you. My truth was that I did. As much as you claimed me. I was yours."

She looked as if he'd punched her in the gut.

When she spoke, her voice was as strangled as if he had. "Are you implying that during our time together you had no one but me?"

"That's not an implication. That's a fact."

She gaped at him as if she'd never heard anything so preposterous.

Heart aching with affront and frustration he hissed,

"What could have possibly raised any doubts about my faithfulness to you?"

That shattered the stasis of incredulity, hardening her eyes and voice again. "Oh, I don't know. Probably the dozens of nubile, and let's not forget to mention 'suitably ranked,' bodies hanging on your arm in every public appearance. While I was safely tucked a world away to be brought out to play with, in secret."

"Those 'bodies' sought me out, because of who I am, not for myself. I didn't want anyone, starting with my mother, to speculate if I rebuffed their public advances. I *told* you that." Disappointment seared through him as he saw it in her eyes. She hadn't considered believing him, then or now. "So you believed I was sleeping around, yet took me back into your arms, welcomed me into your body when I came back to you?"

"Pathetic, isn't it? What's more sickening is that I would have indefinitely put up with being one of your steady stream of exchangeable bodies if I wasn't the only one you wouldn't stoop to associating with in public. Now you know that my anger and disgust weren't all directed toward you."

His lips twisted. "You gifted me with more than enough of it. You started by leaving me, then turned Patrick against me...."

Her eyes turned to steel at Patrick's mention. "It was your unethical business practices that cultivated his enmity, not me."

Everything inside him went still, to ward off yet another unexpected and unearned blow. "He told you that?"

Her gaze wavered. No. Patrick hadn't told her that. She would have said yes if she could. But she couldn't lie—for Patrick. She wouldn't mind saying anything to hurt *him*.

Was all this hatred for him? Or was he paying the collective price for his family?

Her shoulders jerked. "Patrick only made me face facts I'd been avoiding for years—about how you manipulated me for your conveniences, made me consent to being one of your...entertainments. I applied your methods with me to your dealings with Patrick and extrapolated his reasons for ending your partnerships. Why else would he have endured all those losses if it wasn't to stop you from manipulating him anymore?"

"How about that he was so jealous of me, he was making sure I was out of your life, even after he was gone?" Bile filled him up to his eyes. "And I thought him a good friend and a man of honor. All the time he'd been plotting to take you away from me. And he did."

"I had to be *with* you in the first place for him to take me away from you. I never was."

"*B'Ellahi,* that's a lie. You were closer to me than any other person in my life."

"*That* is a testimony to how superficial it all was. You're light-years distant from everyone in your life. You have formed no closeness with anyone starting with your twin. As for what we shared, it was nothing resembling a relationship."

"What did you think I was doing with you for four years, if that wasn't a relationship?"

"Anyone hearing you saying *four years* over and over would think we lived together or something. Do you know how many days out of those four years we had together?"

His heart compressed at yet another proof of how differently they'd perceived the past, how much she held against him that he'd been unaware of. "You counted?"

"Not at the time, but I went back and looked over my schedule, and all the last-minute cancellations I had to make when you had an opening and could grace me with your presence. You acted with the conviction that my life and commitments were of no consequence, and the only one who should be accommodated at the drop of a hat was you."

"You never told me you had to cancel plans to be with me."

She gave a furious laugh. "So you didn't listen when I did. Or you did and it only fed your ego, that I'd drop everything, at whatever cost to me, to jump back in bed with you."

Had they both lived through the same past? Or was she talking about some parallel earth to his?

"I believed you only rescheduled. You never made it sound important, so I assumed your plans were flexible, unlike mine."

"*And* he says that with a straight face. Wow. You're really something. You assumed that I, a struggling model trying to build a name for myself in a sea of women with better qualifications and looks, had the luxury of canceling shoots or even rescheduling them? While you, the prince whom everyone would sacrifice their firstborn for a handshake from, couldn't change your plans at your whim? If you gave it a moment's thought you would have seen the truth, but you didn't bother. You had everything compartmentalized for your convenience. Your business and power games, your sports tournaments, your political and promotional schmoozing, and when you needed to unwind in a sex marathon, you called me, expected me to be there where and when you dictated. And self-degrading fool that I was, I was there. Every single time."

A kaleidoscope of agony spun inside him at her every slashing word. "So you thought I didn't care about you one way or another, thought I'd feel the same about the child you bore me. So why didn't you tell me anyway? Just to make sure? Why were you so anxious to divert me from the truth?"

Sarcasm emptied from her eyes, discomfort replacing

it. "Because this way Adam remained mine alone and your reaction to his existence wouldn't…taint him. I thought if you knew and rejected him, he'd somehow feel it. *I* didn't want to make that rejection real, and it would only be real if you knew.…"

Her words petered out, her cream complexion blotching with crimson agitation.

"So *this* was how you rationalized it all. You painted me as exploitative, cheating scum so you could walk out on me with a clear conscience. Then you condemned me as an unfeeling monster so you could justify depriving me of my *child*."

Silence crashed after his last butchered growl.

Nothing fractured its suffocation but the sounds of his thundering heartbeats and her labored breathing.

Then she croaked, "You—you're really upset?"

"Upset?" A mirthless laugh shredded out of him. *"Upset?"*

His laugh died. He pressed his fist against his chest where it felt it had been ripped open.

She stared up at him, horror settling into her eyes by degrees. "I—I really…really believed it would be the last thing you'd want, to know you had a baby, from me. Y-you did walk out that day saying you'd delete me from your memory."

"You'd just told me that you hated me, hated yourself when you were with me. You said that after I told you how I couldn't forget you, after we almost died of pleasure in each other's arms. What did you expect me to say? If you'd given me any hope, I would have never given up. And if you'd told me when you found out you were pregnant with Adam…" A lump pushed its way up his throat.

"Wh-what would you have done if I'd told you?"

"*Ya Ullah,* what *wouldn't* I have done? Had I been the

second one to know that you carried my child, as I should have been, I would have been there with you, *for* you, for *him,* every moment of the past twenty-eight months. And you deprived me of all that."

The silver of her eyes dimmed until it was eclipsed in a wave of reddened realization and blackening contrition.

Suddenly she staggered around and collapsed on the couch.

"I didn't realize, never believed..." She dropped her face into her palms on a hiccuped gasp.

He looked down at her, witnessing the distress shaking her frame, chopping her breathing for the first time. His own was wildfire that razed through his every nerve.

He walked to her slowly, feeling if he went any faster, he'd keel over. He went down on his knees before her.

She gasped as he took her clammy, trembling hands in his. Tears streaked a pale track down the velvet of her flushed cheeks as she raised her face level with his. Her lips contorted to form words, her voice a thick, tear-clogged tremolo. "Oh, God, I'm so sorry, Jalal...."

One hand pressed against her lips, silencing the flow of her regret. He couldn't bear her apologies. He didn't think he deserved them. Didn't want them even if he did.

He needed only one thing. "I want to see my son, Lujayn. Take me to him. Now."

Eight

Lujayn snatched her hand from his, heaved up to her feet and wiped away the tears that had abruptly stopped. "I can't do that."

He rose to stand, feeling as unsteady as she seemed. His lips and heart compressed on the anger condensing inside him. "Even now, you still persist in trying to deprive me of my son? *Zain, kaif ma tebbi*—as you wish. I only asked you as a courtesy. I don't need your permission or your co-operation to see my son. I'll go to your uncle's to see him, right now."

She lunged at him, caught his arm in a frantic grasp, her face urgent. "You can't. They have no idea you're his father."

A suspicion skewered him in the chest. "You told them he was Patrick's?"

Her color rose into the danger zone. "N-no, they knew he couldn't have been Adam's father. I—I told them it was someone else, but it wasn't important who he was."

Would everything she said keep hurting more? "And they just accepted that?"

She winced. "My father's side of the family did. My mother's, being conservative Azmaharians, were mortified. They rationalized my 'lapse' by my grief, and placated themselves that I'd make it…lawful. When I told them there was no hope of that and I'd decided to keep the baby and would disappear from their lives forever if they couldn't deal with it, they eventually succumbed."

"Decided to keep the baby?" He caught her by the shoulders, each heartbeat a wrecking ball inside his chest. "You considered…terminating your pregnancy?"

"No." Her eyes filled again. "It was a shock to find myself pregnant, under the circumstances, but no matter how difficult I knew it would be, how it would change my life forever, I wanted Adam more than I wanted to live."

A mixture of overwhelming sweetness and bitterness, of longing and regret, expanded inside his chest. He wanted to crush her into him, assuage the alienation, wanted to push her away feeling her nearness would cause him permanent injury.

He did neither, kept holding her at arm's length.

Then he rasped, "Do you have photos?"

"O-of Adam?" Her eyes widened, brightened as if he'd handed her a lifeline. She stumbled out of his hold and to her purse, produced her phone, her hands trembling as she accessed her photos. "I should have thought of this."

She thought he'd be satisfied with seeing his son in photos.

His hand covered the phone's screen as she extended it to him. This wouldn't be how he'd first lay eyes on his son.

"Photos of yourself. When you were pregnant."

The relief on her face drained as hard as her arm fell to

her side. "I wasn't in any condition to think of posing for photos. I'd decided to have Adam, but I wasn't exactly..."

"Happy?"

She shook her head, her eyes filling with the days of anxiety and anguish she'd lived, a woman becoming a single mother.

Suddenly it was vital for him to find something out. "Did you stay in the Hamptons during your pregnancy?"

He'd known from Fadi's reports that she'd put the mansion up for sale around the time she must have given birth. He'd had Fadi acquire it for him, through a third party so she wouldn't refuse to sell. Now, imagining her there, pregnant with his child in Patrick's house, was another turn of the lance embedded in his gut.

"Leaving the mansion and leaving the States was the first thing I did after I discovered my pregnancy. I was too high profile there, and I didn't want anyone finding out."

"By anyone, you mean me."

Her exhalation was laden with resignation. "Actually, you weren't my main concern. Your mother was."

His mother's mention, when he least expected it, was another blow out of blue sky. "Why would you have worried about her?"

"Because she would have realized it's your baby."

"Why would she have?" Confusion screeched inside his head, picking up momentum, churning his thoughts to a sickening mess. "She had no more access to you after your mother left her service, probably never had any interest in you to start with. Why would she have followed your news? And if she had, you'd been married, and she couldn't have found out the exact stage of your pregnancy." He shook his head. "What am I saying? She wouldn't have suspected a thing even had she known the baby wasn't Patrick's. There'd been no reason for her to suspect me being the father. She knew nothing about us."

"She knew everything."

The quiet assertion went off in his head. Time slowed, filled with the debris of the history he'd thought he'd lived as each fragment flew in his face, crashed into him with the force of realization.

His mother had known.

But how? Did he want to know? He'd found out enough crimes his family had perpetrated against hers. Could he bear knowing more?

Aih. He owed it to her, to them, to his son, to know everything, set straight as much of it as he could.

Yet… "I find it impossible to believe she'd known about us and hadn't done something about it."

Her body and expression tensed defensively. "You can believe what you like."

"I am not disbelieving you, I'm…boggled that she knew and just…let us be. She was the main reason I kept us such a heavily guarded secret. She had a way of making anyone we ever came close to…disappear. Admittedly, it was worse with Haidar, *qorrat enha*—the apple of her eye, and she was downright vicious in what she'd done to Roxanne. But I am still her son, and I knew she'd do the same to anyone I came close to that she didn't approve of. And she approved of no one. But when it came to you…"

Her lush lips twisted. "Yeah, her servant's daughter."

"You were never that to *me*. But I knew you were that to her, warranting a whole new level of disapproval if she knew, and consequently an even more…creative intervention."

Her eyes cleared of the rawness of agitation, filled with the mist of contemplation. "You thought she'd harm my family?"

He let out his breath on a ragged exhalation. "I didn't even want to think what she might do if she knew."

Her shrug was dismissive, assertive. "She knew. She told me."

He should be getting used to the constant turmoil being with Lujayn created. If he hadn't till now, he never would.

"And she never did anything," he said. "All right, there goes another corner pillar of my belief system."

"She didn't think she had to do a thing. She thought you were taking care of not sullying your image or family name with such an abominable liaison well enough. She commended you for knowing what my kind was good for, and keeping me where I belonged, in the dark, unacknowledged and reviled."

His blood burned cell by cell as every vicious word that reeked of authenticity bludgeoned him.

He had no doubt those had been his mother's words. What remained to know was... "When did she tell you that?"

She attempted a shrug of nonchalance, failed miserably. "Oh, a bit over six years ago."

When she'd started being contentious and ill-tempered. Now he knew the reason, he thought it a miracle she hadn't walked out on him on that same day. That it had taken her two more years of what must have looked like proof of his mother's words.

So his mother had managed to spoil another vital thing to him. In an even more evil and damaging way than he'd feared.

"It wasn't true, what she said," he finally rasped. "I am now realizing my actions could have been interpreted in a way to validate everything she'd said, and I bet she was counting on that, too, but none of it was in any way true."

Her arms went around her body, as if hugging herself against sudden cold. "She was so proud of what you'd done to me. She said you did what she'd promised me she'd do one day, put me in my place."

"When did she say *that*?"

"Ten years before I met you."

This time it was he who staggered around to find the nearest surface to collapse on.

Lujayn had been only eleven when his mother had threatened her.

After sitting down with the stiff care of someone who had trouble coordinating her movements, she said, "On one of her trips to the States, she called my mother. My mother was in turmoil over answering her 'summons' but she buckled under her conditioning and went. She took me with her. Without inviting us to sit, your mother demanded that she leave her family and come back to her service.

"God, I've never seen Mom like that, couldn't imagine that my vivacious, outspoken mother could stand before anyone so shaken and unable to stand up for herself. She stood there, head bent, taking your mother's cruelty as she hacked at her, saying she'd deserted her in a pathetic attempt for independence that only landed her with a slob of a husband who'd never be out of debt. That she'd gone from a highly paid lady-in-waiting to a queen to the servant of a bum and his children for free. I saw my mother shriveling under her barrage, and I couldn't bear it."

He couldn't either. Was there no end to his mother's transgressions? Had he ever had a chance with Lujayn? He must have always been inextricable in her mind from his mother, and her feelings toward him had no doubt been tainted by his mother's degradation of hers. Then she went on, and he realized there was always worse than the worst he could think of.

"I put myself in front of my mother, as if I'd protect her from your mother's attack. My mother tried to stop me, but

I walked up to your mother and told her I never thought anyone could be as beautiful as her. Or as mean. I told her she was scary and ugly inside and that my mother left her because she made her miserable like she made others, and that everyone hated her. And I could see why. Then I told my mother that I wouldn't let her go back to work for this woman, that I'll give up everything, my ballet and piano lessons and get work to help her."

He could see her, a slip of a girl, standing up to his dragoness of a mother, to defend her family. His heart slowed to a painful thud as she went on.

"Your mother looked at me in contemplation all through my tirade. Then she said that as a princess from birth, then a queen by marriage, it was her duty to maintain order, restore balance. She took it upon herself to put people in their correct places. But to do so, it took time and patience, so she was not in any hurry. But she never forgot her purpose, refused to stop until she saw it through. And she would put me in my place, no matter how long it took, since I clearly had no idea what it was."

He wanted to shout, *enough!* But he knew it wasn't, not for her. She had to let this all out once and for all.

Gritting his teeth on the sharpening pain in his chest, he willed her to go on.

She did. "But I was too young and didn't believe anyone would be as vindictive and long-term as that. Mom begged Sondoss to please forgive us, me for my foolishness and her for not being able to leave her family. Sondoss only said my mother would change her mind, when life with us, her miserable family, became impossible.

"Mom was a wreck as we left, and remained one for the next year. Dad lost his latest job, and couldn't find another. Soon, what had been a barely manageable situation became impossible as per your mother's predictions. Mom had to go back to her service, while Dad had to go back to his family in Ireland. Mom took my younger sister and brother, while Dad took me, tearing apart our family. Dad asked Mom to take me, too, said I shouldn't be away from my mother and siblings. But it wasn't for him that Mom let me go. She knew if she took me with her, your mother would find ways to 'put me in my place.' I cried for days, begging her to take me with her, saying I would do anything to make your mother forgive me. But she knew. Your mother never forgot, or forgave. So your infallible memory comes from both sides of your heritage."

He'd already known his mother had orchestrated a conspiracy that could have only played out in endless bloodshed. Why would he consider this premeditated cruelty any more shocking?

But it was. Her conspiracy had been, to her, justified, to give her sons, those she considered the ones worthy of being kings, the thrones they deserved. What she'd done to Lujayn and her mother had been nothing but pure malice.

Lujayn angrily wiped at the fresh flow of tears. "But Mom promised it would only be for a couple years. Sondoss was a slave driver, but she paid her servants very well. Mom estimated she'd be able to put aside the capital Dad needed to start the business he'd always dreamed of. But as if knowing Mom's plan in advance, your mother offered a salary only large enough to support us and pay a portion of our debts."

His mother *had* known. She had a way of knowing everything. And using it to her advantage. To everybody else's loss.

The voice that had steadied began to shake again. "Dad kept losing every job he got, to his growing despair. He'd think he was doing so well then he'd be let go. He believed he was jinxed."

A jinx called Sondoss. This had his mother's claws all over it. No need to draw her attention to that conclusion if she hadn't reached it herself. Nothing to be gained from infecting her soul with even more rage and hatred.

"I did give up everything I was involved in, started to work when I was fourteen. But by the time I was eighteen, I knew the jobs I kept getting were hand-to-mouth solutions. There was no way I could afford college and even if I could, I couldn't wait for the well-paying jobs a degree would afford me. I needed something that didn't take long training, something that would pay well fast. I had nothing to use but 'my body' as you put it. I always had people complimenting my 'exotic' looks, saying I could be a model. But it wasn't as easy as that. It took me a whole year before I landed my first paying job. It paid enough to buy a new outfit to wear to auditions, and a bottle of cheap champagne to celebrate with Dad. Not that there was much to celebrate.

"I was exposed to some…scary situations. People started coming out of the woodwork, wanting to be my 'agent,' 'manager' or 'entourage.' I'd just decided to admit defeat and get the first shop-clerk job I could find, when I met Aliyah again and told her I saw why she'd left modeling. She offered to help financially first, but when I refused she decided to teach me to 'fish.' She took me under her wing, showed me the ropes, introduced me to the right people and I started working, making money, started paying our debts, and I thought my life was finally on the right track. Then I met you."

His eyes squeezed without volition. The way she'd said that. What he considered the best memory of his life, she considered the worst. Forcing his eyes open, so he'd see for himself how totally wrong he'd been about everything he'd ever shared with her, he watched her struggle to continue her account.

"I was horrified. You were the son of my mother's enslaver, a part of the reason I didn't have my family in my life, and might never have them. To my mortification, I found you fascinating. I'd seen you so many times from afar before that…."

"You did?"

"I'd been in Azmahar many times to visit Mom, when your mother was too busy. Then after that first meeting, after every exposure, I found myself unable to think of anything else but you. I told myself I'd have some more time with you before the inevitable end, because the moment I told you who I was, you'd be the one to walk away."

"And you told me."

"Yeah. And instead of coming to your senses as I thought you would, you decided to have your cake and eat it, too. And it kept eating at me, how I wanted you, when I shouldn't.

"At first, it was because I couldn't let my family find out about you. I felt I was betraying them, not only by being with the son of the woman who'd torn us apart, but because I was acting like anything but the person they'd raised. I was ashamed of the way I breathlessly did anything you even hinted at, accommodated your whims at my expense. I cut myself off from them because I couldn't bear the shame of lying to them with every breath, since that was how frequently I thought of you.

"Then your mother validated all my suspicions and far more—and you kept proving her right. I despised myself, escalating those feelings every day because of the way I let you treat me, and I still couldn't quit you. Then I really started hating what I had become when I kept inventing quarrels with you, hoping to nudge you into addressing the issues that were poisoning me. I was too much of a coward to face you with them, out of fear that you'd just shrug and say, 'If this bothers you, tough,' and walk away. So I started to self-destruct. I couldn't eat, couldn't sleep, kept obsessing over every day you didn't call, every minute you stayed away. I lost weight and jobs. I was on the verge of losing my mind. And I didn't have any support system to fall back on, since I'd shut everyone out. I felt I had to choose between being with them or being with you.

"I chose you, and lost everything. The one person I had left, the only one I could talk to, was Patrick. And he stepped in and gave me the support I needed to save myself."

And she fell silent. He knew she had no more to say.

She'd said enough.

He threw back his head against the couch, closed his eyes, suppressing the chaos that threatened to tear him apart, soul and psyche.

Finally he opened his eyes, rose and walked to her, holding her raw, stormy gaze. Then he went down on his knees before her again.

He gently aborted her jerk to get away, taking her hands in his. "You should have told me everything long ago. What I have to say is not much, but it's all I have, for now.

"I can't begin to describe my shame and regret at what my mother stole of your childhood and family life, what she told you about me and the cost to both of us. But I was never party to her manipulations, was never tainted by her snobbery. I was *never* ashamed of you—I was the very opposite, and this had nothing to do with the secrecy I imposed on our relationship. I thought there would be only losses and trouble if the world knew what we had.

"I also thought we had the perfect arrangement, the best of all worlds. We were young, were building our careers and we had each other. I didn't think there was anything more than that to dream of. I was ignorant of the true history between our families, didn't realize you came to our relationship with baggage and insecurities and bitterness. But

I should have realized something was deeply wrong when you started flaring up, shouldn't have rationalized it because I was content with the way things were. At the time, I did think you appreciated the secrecy as much as I did for your family's conservative sensibilities, and so you wouldn't be dragged into the crosshairs of the paparazzi who hounded me. I welcomed having those women on my arm because they diverted attention from you, kept you safe. But I was yours alone, Lujayn…." Something still stopped him from admitting that he'd never stopped being hers, would never stop. "And I believed you were mine. That's why I went out of my mind when you left me for Patrick. Anything I did with him, anything I said to you, was fueled by my pain and jealousy. I was blind and I hurt you just the same as if I'd meant to. And for that, I will never forgive myself, will do anything so you can have the peace I robbed you of all these years."

Her features trembled and she pitched forward to bury her face in her hands, ended up pressing it into their entwined fingers. Her flesh, her tears, singed him, had him groaning, dragging her to his chest. She burrowed her face into him, rubbing against him like a cat desperate for her human's feel and affection, her lips over his heart.

His hands felt like they didn't belong to him as they fumbled his shirt buttons open, needing that touch like he needed his next heartbeat. Her moan against his flesh as those petal-soft lips crushed their lushness into him was a bolt of pure emotion and carnality, striking him dead center through his being.

His fingers tangled into her silken tresses, dug into her scalp, shaping her beloved head. Her moans grew longer, louder, confessing her equal upheaval as she opened her lips and the wet heat of her tongue scalded him. That simmering state of arousal she had him in by just existing, that had been hovering on the verge of igniting with her nearness, exploded into a conflagration that consumed him body and soul.

He crushed her to him, the starved for feel of her sending his senses spiraling beyond retrieval. He took all he could of her worshipping, before a hand at her nape raised her to him, brought her roving, tormenting lips up to his, bit down into the lower one, almost breaking the inner flesh in his urgency. His teeth held there as he trembled all over like she did, with the effort of holding back. Her cry razed through him as she opened fully to him, her ripe breasts pressing into his chest, demanding his domination. He laved away his bite, thrust his tongue inside her, draining her sweetness and whimpers of pleasure. His kisses grew wrenching as he pushed away her jacket, dipped beneath her blouse to spread his hands over the scorching velvet of her back, arching her against him.

He poured his demand, his plea, his confession, into her depths. *"Wahashtini ya'yooni, bejnoon. Guleeli ya rohi, wahashtek? Tebghini kamma abghaki?"*

"Yes, Jalal, yes...I've been going insane with missing you, craving you, too. How I missed you—*how* I crave you...."

That was all he needed. The license to claim her, reclaim them both from the desert they'd existed in without the other's passion and fulfillment.

In one movement, he was on his feet with his woman in his arms. But when he neared the room's door she gasped, wriggled. His lips buried into her neck. "We're alone."

His reassurance defused her tension, had her resume owning any inch of flesh he'd exposed to her.

In a minute he took her across the threshold of the expansive bedroom suite where he'd lain awake, burning in a hell of deprivation, for the past weeks. Her teeth were scraping his stubble as he placed her on the bed. He straddled her hips and started to rid her of those prim clothes that had been playing havoc with his imagination, had her naked in what felt like a torturous hour. Then he pulled back to look down at her.

Her breasts were a feast, her hips flared with fertility, making her waist look more nipped, her belly no longer flat, but a lush curve, her arms round and firm, her legs long and smooth and honey-hued, her mound plump and trimmed.

He followed all those treasures, in sweeps of wonder. "You robbed me of my sanity from the moment I saw you, when you were nothing like what you've become. Now— now I'm in danger of devouring you for real. *Ya Ullah, Lujayn*...what have you done to yourself? Nothing should be this beautiful."

"Don't exaggerate—I've put on too much weight...."

"There can't be too much of you for me. You were slim, then you became almost gaunt, not that it made me want you any less. But now..." He skimmed a coveting hand from the curve of her strong, square shoulder to her heavy breast, blood roaring in his ears, his loins, as its warmth and resilience overflowed in his large hand. "Now you're beyond glorious. My silver-eyed enchantress has become a goddess."

She thrust her breast into his hold, inviting a more aggressive possession. "You were always a god, now you've become something even more."

He bent to award himself with compulsive suckles of her peach-colored, erect nipples, groaning at her taste and feel, as she pushed her flesh deeper into his mouth, whimpering her greed for more as she treated his clothes as he'd treated hers.

Delight expanded through him as he surrendered to her impatience, wallowing in it as she exposed him to her hunger.

He came down on top of her, plundering her fragrant mouth in savage kisses, his hands seeking all her secrets, taking every license, owning every inch. His fingers sought her molten depths, delighted in feeling them clamp around him in demand, as she keened and undulated beneath him, accepting the pleasure, inviting him with movements and words to do whatever he wished to her. She was too ready, as she always was for him; he brought her to orgasm around his fingers with just a few thrusts.

As she shook with that warm-up pleasure, he slid down the bed, draped her legs over his shoulders. She wantonly arched her hips, opening herself wide for his devouring. Her taste and scent blanketed his sanity as he lost all sense of self, becoming a beast bent on drinking his mate dry. And he did, while he suckled and tongued her to two more climaxes, his growls inhuman as he drained her overflowing pleasure.

She lay melted beneath him, aftershocks discharging through her as he rose above her. Her hands shook as they delighted in shaping and feeling him. Though his mind was unraveling, he let her own him like he'd just owned her. But when her hands wrapped around his now-painful erection, and her tongue licked her lips, miming her intentions, he stopped her.

Her eyes flared and subsided with that hypnotic light, her flush intensifying it. "Not fair. You had your way with me...."

"You'll have your way with me, whenever and however you want. Just not now. This time I need to be inside you." Something penetrated the fog of lust wrapping his mind. "But if you're not..."

She shook her head against the light gray sheets that echoed her eyes and deepened the gloss of her raven hair, opening her thighs wide for him. "It's safe. Come inside me, Jalal, just fill me, with yourself, with your pleasure."

"Lujayn." He could swear he heard something snap, crumble. The last shred of restraint.

He snatched up her silken legs, hooking her ankles around his neck, the only position where he could plumb deepest inside her, where she almost accommodated him. He cupped her buttocks, mounted her, then holding her focus, groaning her name, he thrust inside her, felt as if he'd plunged into a vise of pure, molten pleasure.

Her scream echoed his roar as her hot flesh stretched for his invasion, her back arched, her whole body trembling like a strummed string with the shock of pain and pleasure. He withdrew, plunged again, seeking to breach her completely as he knew she needed him to, sensation slashing through him. Another sharp keen squeezed out of her depths as she smashed herself against him, seeking his full domination. He gave it to her, forging deeper with every thrust. She orgasmed over and over, shrieks shredding her voice, convulsions racking her whole body beneath his and her inner muscles around his girth.

He waited until pleasure was electrifying her in a continuous current, squeezing him beyond insanity, then erupted in his own release, his buttocks contracting into her cradle, his erection buried to the hilt inside her quivering flesh. He held himself at her womb as his seed seared through his length in jet after jet of excruciating pleasure.

Somewhere in his brain thoughts floated among the lethargy of satisfaction. The last time they'd had such profound fulfillment in each other, a life had been created, their son. And if it wasn't safe as she thought, this time another miracle might happen, another son, or better still a daughter....

He lurched back into the present, found himself spread beneath the warm, satiated embodiment of all his desires.

His heart contracted with remembrance. The last time this had happened, she'd broken away from him, her eyes cold and reviling. He couldn't survive it this time if she…

She purred something, a sound of total satisfaction, secured him in a more intimate embrace. Everything inside him fell apart in relief, in thankfulness, as he luxuriated in gliding his hands over her lushness, grinding his unabated arousal against that belly that had borne him his son. She turned her face up at him, opened for him as their mouths mated again and again.

As she dived back into his hold, his gaze fell on the wall clock. It was 1:00 a.m.

Uzeem. Great. By the time he had her in any shape that didn't say "savagely pleasured female," it might be dawn. He couldn't return her to her family looking like that, eyes barely open, mouth swollen, skin flushed with simmering lust.

He sighed, deciding this was too incredible to waste any of it worrying. He'd somehow iron this out with her family. For now, he'd savor each breath and nuance of this reunion. This revival.

He hugged her tighter, arms and legs. She sighed in bone-deep bliss, melted deeper into his full-body embrace.

He sighed again, brought up the only other thing he had on his mind anymore. "I want to see Adam tomorrow. Make that today."

She raised a wobbling head, her blissful expression receding, resurging tension clamping her every muscle. "I can't, Jalal."

He stiffened, didn't stop her when she struggled to sit up.

Her eyes pleaded as she looked at him. "I'm not contesting your right to see Adam. But I won't turn my family's life upside down while I'm here. It will be difficult enough to explain away tonight."

Unable to bear her agitation, wanting only to alleviate her worries, he brought her back to him in a searing kiss, whispered against her lips, "Then you bring him to me."

Nine

"Do you realize how huge this is?"

Lujayn winced at the nerve-fraying excitement in her younger sister's exclamation.

She ignored her as she tried to talk Adam out of wriggling down from her arms to run up the cut-stone path toward Jalal's villa on his own.

Dahab pounced on Adam, took him from her, distracting him with whooping tickles. Adam shrieked, delighted with his favorite playmate's antics. It made Lujayn realize again that while she was the one he reached for in almost everything, he never laughed with her as wholeheartedly. She hadn't been as playful with her son as she should have been. She'd let the circumstances of his birth dim her spirits, though she'd been determined not to. Seemed in spite of her best intentions and efforts, she had shortchanged him.

Now she was entering a new level of turmoil, with Jalal

invading her life on all frontiers…as he'd invaded *her* last night.…

God, what he'd done to her! She'd been in a state of molten agony ever since. She'd thought she'd remembered in distressing detail the pleasure he'd wrung from her, had even exaggerated it. Turned out she'd downplayed it. Had he always been this…?

"Huge! As in *humongous!*" Dahab exclaimed again, securing Adam on her hip. "You and Prince Overwhelming himself! Man, is this going to blow millions of hopeful females' dreams to smithereens when they know he's taken!"

Biting back a retort that he wasn't, so those millions could still hope, she kept her tone sweet for Adam's benefit. "Dahab—shut *up*. You're making me sorrier by the second that I told you."

Her impish sister stuck out her tongue at her. Adam followed suit, then burst into giggles again. Lujayn groaned. Dahab might be a fun companion for Adam, but she was no role model. Anyone would think she was twelve not twenty-two.

"First, you had to tell me. You needed me as a decoy because otherwise everyone would have wondered why you're taking Adam out when you've been leaving him with me for weeks. Second, you should be sorry indeed. How could you keep it from me—*me*—that Adam is Prince Jalal's?" Dahab swung up Adam. "No wonder you're the most gorgeous boy on earth. You take after your father."

Lujayn grimaced. Great. Even her own sister was infatuated with Jalal. But then, what female with a pulse wouldn't be?

But he'd taken her last night as if he'd been suffocating and she'd been air. Or maybe she'd reflected her feelings on him…

"I mean, I understand not telling Mom and the rest of

the Al—oops, *Aal* Ghamdi clan, what with their fourteenth-century brains. But *me?*" Dahab squinted at Adam. "Can you believe it, you edible tyke? She didn't tell *me!*"

"I'm still wondering how you lived your formative years here and didn't develop the basic persona. But you did develop the modern *me, me, me* one, didn't you?" Lujayn smirked as she slowed down more, loath to reach their destination.

She didn't know how she'd face Jalal again, what his reaction would be to Adam and Adam's to him. She'd brought Dahab to defuse the situation with her lighthearted vivaciousness.

"Actually, I'm all about you, *you*—" Dahab squeezed Adam "—and *him,* right now."

Lujayn gave her a warning/pleading look. "Speaking of *him,* you will attempt not to voice every thought and question that flits in your mind, right?"

Dahab feigned indignation. "Hey, I'm not *that* bad!" Then she wiggled her eyebrows. "But don't worry. I'm here to take a close-up look at the Prince of Many Gorgeousnesses and witness this historic meeting between father and son, but I won't stay. Got a hot date at two."

Great. So she'd get the disadvantage of her unpredictability without the advantage of her presence.

For the rest of the way, Lujayn looked around the grounds she'd barely noticed last night. Without Jalal's presence blinding her, she realized the place was like a mini-oasis. Teeming palm trees surrounded the periphery. Beyond that, the grounds were landscaped in mini-dunes and lawns with breathtaking beds of desert plants in the shadow of more palm trees of all shapes. A huge crescent-shaped *ein*—spring sparkled emerald and curved around the central two-level sprawling residence crouching on the most elevated dune and overlooking the desert that stretched into the horizon. The villa itself was a masterpiece in modern elegance and exotic design with an amalgam of Arab, Ottoman and Persian influences.

And as per Jalal's promise, the place was deserted, to assure their privacy. At some point up the winding path to the veranda where she'd entered the villa last night, Adam threw himself into her arms again in order to point things out, curious to know everything.

She was explaining about the *ein,* and debating with Dahab whether it was natural or artificial when suddenly nothing was left, in her mind, in the world.

Jalal was striding across the veranda eagerly. She was grateful for Dahab's presence when the sight of her slowed him down. But it was only seconds before they reached him where he stood at the top of the stairs, the intensity in his eyes almost evaporating her, even when it was, for once, not directed to her.

All his being was focused on Adam.

The next minutes, as father and son looked at each other in total stillness and silence, were the most tempestuously emotional of her life.

It felt as if all the months since the day Adam had been conceived were compacted, everything she'd felt and thought and suffered condensing in her heart, almost imploding it.

Holding in the tremors and tears with all she had, she watched the two people who possessed the lion's share of her heart and soul and destiny.

Adam, who was never still while awake, remained motionless, all his faculties trained at that larger-than-life entity who was looking at him as if nothing in the world existed but him. Having been born within an extended family, Adam was used to being around people, to accepting new ones. But he'd never reacted that way to someone new. To anyone. She could see it, sense it. He just knew Jalal was different from anyone else. And it wasn't because he was the largest man he'd ever seen, or who emitted the most power. She could swear she could feel, almost *taste* the bond that existed between them. It arced out of each, caught her in the cross fire before it sank into the other, transforming them all forever.

Suddenly, Jalal moved, fracturing the unbearably poignant moment, and almost her tenuous coordination and consciousness. Her sight blurred as Jalal reached a hand that visibly shook to feather a touch laden with awe down Adam's cheek.

"*Ya Ullah, ya* Lujayn—*ya Ullah!* Our son!"

The thick, ragged wonder in his voice, the agonized delight gripping his face, had her heart quivering, her nerves firing haphazardly, each jolt a tiny electrocution.

She'd never even let herself imagine this moment. She'd refused to paint scenarios of what he'd do, how he'd feel, if he saw Adam when he knew he was his. She'd strangled any thought before it came to life. Because any imagining would have been a shard embedded in her heart, an injury that would have constantly bled and drained her of life and will.

"*Ma ajmalak men subbi. Enta mo' jezah!*"

What a beautiful boy you are. You're a miracle.

"*Baba?*"

Adam's chirping voice articulated the word softly, carefully. It detonated in her head and heart, snapped her control. Tears poured, squeezed from her very essence.

Jalal's eyes, struck and reddened, tore from Adam to her, their question dazed but clear. She shook her head. She hadn't told Adam anything. But Adam knew other kids had their *babas.* He'd recognized Jalal as his.

A shudder shook through Jalal's great body, tears filled his wolf eyes as a smile she'd never thought to see trembled on his lips, one of heartbreaking tenderness. "*Aih, ya sugheeri, ana Baba."* One finger touched Adam over his heart. *"W'enta ebni."*

Yes, my little one, I'm your father. And you're my son.

Then he held out his arms to Adam.

A whimper escaped her as emotion spiked, twisting her insides. Adam always checked with her, asking her consent in a smile or a verbal encouragement, before he let a new person hold him. He asked for none now, pitched himself into Jalal's arms.

A groan of overwhelmed joy and relief rumbled from Jalal as he received Adam's robust body with care and reverence.

Adam pointed to himself, said his name, had Jalal repeating it after him before he proceeded to name his articles of clothing. Then examining Jalal with utmost concentration and interest, he pawed his face and triumphantly named his features. Satisfied with his preliminary exploration, he smiled at Jalal shyly, produced his precious pink elephant from his pocket.

As Jalal accepted it, looking more moved than she had thought possible, she heard Dahab's voice as if coming from another realm.

"You should consider yourself privileged beyond imagining. No one, and I mean *no* one is allowed to even touch Mimi."

Smiling with his whole body, Jalal turned to Dahab. "I assure you, I feel far more than that. I feel blessed for the first time in my life, when I in no way deserve to be." He reached out one of those immaculate hands to her. Adam squeaked out her name. Jalal chuckled. "Thanks for the introduction, *ya sugheeri*. I certainly see why your aunt was called that."

Dahab was Lujayn's very opposite in coloring, with hair of pure gold, hence her name, and dark chocolate eyes.

As Jalal shook Dahab's hand, his eyes warm and his smile warmer, a sick frisson went through Lujayn. In spite of her bravado, Dahab was fluttering under Jalal's influence, and she was also the most beautiful woman Lujayn had ever seen. What if…

Jalal swung his gaze back to Adam, looking down in awe at the upturned cherubic face that looked back at him with the same fascination. At length, he let out a ragged exhalation, looked at her for real for the first time today.

"*Ya Ullah, ya* Lujayn, what is this miraculous being we managed to have between us? This prodigy who recognized me on sight?" He grinned at Adam, squeezed and tickled him. "So who am I? Who am I, you most wonderful and intelligent tot? Let me hear it again."

Adam wriggled his excitement, shrieked his delight. *"Baba!"*

"That's right, you magnificent boy, you! I am *Baba* Jalal. Can you say that?"

"Baba Jalal!"

Jalal's eyelashes fluttered, as if blinking back tears. "*Ya Ullah,* I didn't even think you'd be able to talk at this age."

"Oh, he talks." Dahab chuckled. "*All* the time. A lot is still in his own language, like 'bandend' for balloon, and 'minkilonti' for macaroni, but he manages to make you get his drift."

"He says fifty-six words, in Arabic and English." Lujayn realized she'd spoken only when they all looked at her. "Uh…I write down everything he says. It's beyond his developmental age, which is fifty words at most, in one language…."

Her voice petered out at the flare of intensity in Jalal's eyes. Suddenly she found herself tucked into his body with Adam. Before she drew another breath, he took her lips in a scorching, devouring kiss that had blood whooshing in torrents in her head.

In the periphery of an awareness that overflowed with sensation, whoops and whistles echoed, until he unlocked the seal of their lips and raised his head to smile at their approving and encouraging audience.

Adam mashed their faces back together. "Kiss, kiss."

"Son, your wish is my command." Jalal chuckled, searing her with another kiss punctuated by the enthusiasm of their son and Dahab.

He released her seconds before she swooned, passion and mirth setting his eyes on golden fire. "You have to give me that list. And another of his own words." She nodded numbly as he looked down at Adam who nestled into him contentedly. Pride blazed in his eyes as he turned them back to her. "How can I ever thank you for the priceless treasure of our son, *ya'yooni'l feddeyah?*"

She almost said something as inane as "You have a fifty-percent share of his pricelessness, so we're even." Only her scrambled speech centers stopped her.

"Whoa, and he's verbal and poetic, too!" Dahab whistled again. "Anything you're not great at, Prince Jalal?"

"Do you want an alphabetized list? From what I've been finding out lately about my mess ups, it might be a good-sized volume." Jalal raised one formidable eyebrow at Dahab. "And just Jalal. If you don't want me to call you Sheikha Dahab."

Dahab shuddered. "Ugh. Reserve that for Mom and Aunt. I still don't know how I'll survive my friends finding out about this little gem of archaic pompousness."

Jalal chuckled. "Is being a sheikha such a terrible thing?"

Dahab quirked her lips at him. "You tell me. How's being a prince been for you so far?"

He sobered, exhaled. "*Aih*. The perks have certainly been

far outweighed by the aggravations, enmities and heart-aches."

"There you go. I'd rather remain plain old Dahab Morgan."

Jalal exhaled. "Seems I owe you an apology for outing your family for the nobility they are."

"Are you kidding? That's the best thing that has ever happened to them and I can't thank you enough on their behalf. Me, I'll just deal with it by being as un-sheikha-like as possible."

Jalal smiled down at Adam, smoothing his hand in wonder over his silken raven hair and his downy-soft face. Lujayn could swear Adam purred in pleasure. "Tell your aunt she'll never owe me any thanks. She needs only to ask anything and it's done. I'm at her command, just as I am at anyone's who loves you."

"Wow. Now I know what Aladdin felt like!"

As if understanding his aunt's quip, Adam burst out giggling, took Jalal's face in his chubby hands and kissed him soundly.

Jalal squeezed his eyes and groaned, looking as if he'd been punched in the gut with a battering ram of emotion.

Dahab chuckled at his distressed expression. "Excuse me, Jalal, but you're behaving as if you've never heard a baby laugh before. Or been kissed by one."

"I've never heard mine laugh or been kissed by him." Jalal hugged Adam closer to his heart, rubbed his face against his silky hair, kissed the top of his head. Realizing he was being worshipped by this huge man, Adam dived more securely into Jalal's embrace as if he'd always been there.

Jalal hugged him and Lujayn tighter, alternated his gaze between their upturned faces, his voice becoming a ragged rasp. "He has your eyes. He has your *everything*. But he somehow also has mine. He makes us look alike."

She gaped at him, then at Adam. Her mouth fell open. He was right. She'd never wanted to see Jalal in Adam, but he was there, in just about everything as he'd said. In the shape of the eyes, the dimples in the cheek, the cleft chin, the hairline, the hair itself. It wasn't hers as she'd always assumed, had the exact hue and shine and wave of Jalal's....

"Now that you've put your finger on it, oh yeah!" Dahab exclaimed. "You two suddenly do look alike, when just a second ago I saw nothing in common between you but that fabulous black hair, which on closer inspection isn't even the same color, after all!"

Right then, Adam decided they'd had enough introductions and exclamations, tapped Jalal's shoulder with a commanding "Down."

Laughing at Adam's nonnegotiable order, and still holding her to his side, Jalal bent and put Adam on the ground. Adam darted toward the open veranda doors.

At the threshold he turned. "Play."

Laughing again, Jalal took both her and Dahab by the shoulders. "The little prince has spoken."

At that humorous declaration, Lujayn's heart dropped a handful of beats. She almost stumbled as Jalal led them inside where he had a sumptuous lunch prepared. He insisted that Dahab postpone her date and have the meal with them.

All through the late lunch, he laughed with Dahab, doted on Lujayn and Adam, and answered Adam's incessant curiosities and demands for his attention with unending patience and unwavering enjoyment. Lujayn barely ate, or participated, upheaval intensifying as realizations piled up.

She hadn't even thought any of this possible. Jalal's response to Adam, the fluency of interaction between them, that instant bond and mutual appreciation and delight. And it left her in an untenable situation, both retroactively and going forward.

She *had* deprived Jalal—both—no, *all* of them of all that. And she couldn't see how she could stop doing it from now on.

The only way she could was if she agreed to Jalal's earlier proposition. After she left Azmahar, he'd come to them whenever he could, to continue their affair and be Adam's father. She had to admit, after what had happened between them last night, after today, there was nothing she wanted more from life.

But that would only be a finite solution. According to her uncle, the throne was almost in Jalal's bag. Once he became king, he'd need a queen and heirs. Legitimate heirs. Which meant their…arrangement would be temporary. And though their relationship would end when he married, his relationship with Adam wouldn't. But it would remain clandestine for his throne's and rightful heirs' sakes. That might be acceptable now, with Adam so young and unaware, but in a few years? She would never let Adam suffer being an unacknowledged, second-class son.

But how could she deprive him of his father now, after she'd seen them together, realized what a difference Jalal would make in Adam's life? While Jalal's duty to the throne would force him not to acknowledge Adam publicly, he would love him, would want to be his father in every other way that mattered.

But would that be enough? Could she make the decision for Adam, when whatever she chose would end up hurting him?

Feeling like she was about to tear down the middle, she barely interacted with the others until Adam napped and Dahab left. And she had nowhere to hide from Jalal's focus.

Before he could say anything to make any coherent thought impossible, she spoke up as soon as he returned from seeing Dahab off. "We have to talk."

His smile sizzled over her as he came closer. "First let me thank you for not telling your sister what a son of an ex-royal bitch I was with you. I bet if you'd told her half the things I did, instead of acceptance and laughter, she would have ripped my head off. And though I don't deserve it, you also didn't influence Adam in any way, either, but let him make up his own mind about me."

The lump that now perpetually occupied her throat expanded. "What happened between us remains between us. And I realize I've misinterpreted a good chunk of it, anyway."

"It still doesn't change the facts of what happened. So I'm deeply grateful that you didn't expose my...wrongdoings."

Her throat closed completely. "I'd never say anything to anyone, and I'd certainly never try to turn Adam against you."

He didn't stop until he had plastered himself against her. "Jalal, please, we need to talk...."

He pulled her fully against him, "And we will. But before anything, we have to do what all parents must always do." He hugged her off the ground, buried his face in her neck. "Make love, hard and fast, before our baby wakes up."

She stood paralyzed as his hands and lips roamed her, worshipping and accessing all her triggers. She drowned in his kiss, his hunger, her body blossoming under his appreciation and ministrations...then a thought detonated in her mind.

She pushed out of his arms. "God, how didn't I think of this?"

He tried to reach for her again, his hands gentle, his eyes concerned. "What is it?"

She stumbled away. "I know Dahab will keep our secret, but how didn't we think of Adam? He's not about to forget this visit."

"I certainly hope he won't!"

"But he'll tell everyone about *Baba* Jalal," she exclaimed.

His face relaxed in such a smile, indulgent and proud. "I certainly hope he would."

She shook her head, implications falling into place, each a new blow. "I'll have to leave Uncle's home and go live in that hotel until we leave Azmahar so he won't be exposed to anyone."

"There's no need for any of that. You can tell everyone now."

She gaped at him. "You know I can't do that. One scandal already consumed most of my family's lives. I won't cause them another. And it's out of the question for *you,* now of all times. With your campaign, the last thing you need is a scandal of the caliber of an illegitimate child."

He took her by the shoulders, his face gripped with fierce emotions. "Adam is not any such thing. He is my son and I'll proclaim him my heir in front of the whole world."

She had no answer to that. For what felt like eternity.

Then she could barely whisper, "Y-you can't do that."

"I can and I will. I have a son and I will be his father, in every way possible."

Suddenly a suspicion spread through her like wildfire. She pushed away his hands as if they burned her. "If you're thinking you can take him from me…"

He raised both hands as if to ward off a blow, his expression agonized. "Don't even complete that thought. *Ya Ullah,* you think I would even consider such a thing?"

She shook her head slowly, confusion rising. "It's just I don't see how else you'd do all…that."

"I will do it the one and only way. We will get married."

Ten

"We can't do that."

Lujayn's ready rejection hit a bull's-eye in Jalal's heart. It hadn't even been an exclamation, but a statement.

His gaze left hers, moved to that miracle that was their son sleeping so peacefully facedown over his thick, colorful blanket on the floor. Adam felt already integrated into his being, as if he'd been a part of him since long before he'd been born. Like she was. Their presence had turned this place into a home. The intensity with which he wanted to claim them, have them with him, forming the most vital parts of his life, was frightening, exhilarating, transfiguring.

But he was just beginning to wrap his mind around what Lujayn had suffered, from childhood up till this day. He didn't have the right to feel bad that her first reaction was to reject the idea of marrying him out of hand, even after she'd made soul-searing love with him last night, and had already borne him Adam.

He had to put her needs as his first and only priority. From now on, everything would be about her. And Adam. About his family.

Emptying his face and voice of any emotion that might push her in the wrong direction, he asked, "Any reason why we can't?"

"How about every reason?"

"I can only see we have every reason to get married. Each other, Adam…"

"We don't have each other, we just slept together a couple times during the last two years."

"I would have been in your bed every night of those two years if you hadn't told me you hated me. It was why I walked away…."

"If you respected or valued me, nothing I said would have made you walk away," she cut him off, her eyes feverish. "But you despised and mistrusted me, when you had no reason to. You felt I betrayed you, but betrayal is when you give something of yourself, and someone takes it and screws you over. You gave me nothing, so what was there to betray? I exercised my right to self-preservation and you came after me, maligning and accusing. And you walked away because you always intended to, never looking back. Then I came here and you wanted to have more no-strings fun. Then you discover Adam and suddenly you want to marry me? I don't think so."

Every word gouged him deeper for being true. "I confess to all my crimes against you, Lujayn. You gave without taking, never gave me reason to mistrust you. You told me why you were leaving, but I couldn't accept it. All I could think of was my disappointment, my pain. The more I thought about it in your absence, the more I twisted everything to soothe my wounds. I am wired to think the worst of everyone first if it would explain their behavior. It comes from having Sondoss for a mother. But I'm never mistrusting you, and I'm never walking away, ever again."

Those ready tears filled her eyes, making them flash like diamonds. "For God's sake, don't even pretend this has anything to do with me. You only want to marry me for Adam."

"Legitimizing Adam is only a factor in the timing but—"

"Did you ever think of marrying me before?"

He wanted to say yes. But there'd never be anything but the whole truth between them from now on. "In the past, I never thought of getting married, no. I thought there was no reason to."

Her lips twisted. "There you go. And there's no reason still."

"I didn't mean it the way you're taking it. You know now I thought we had it all. I didn't think marriage was in either of our horizons. We were too busy, and I thought you were too young, and with your career, wouldn't afford the distraction of marriage let alone the responsibility of a family."

Her eyes narrowed to silver lasers. "Are you saying you did think of marriage and decided against it?"

"I'm saying I didn't think of it for all those reasons, not the ones you're implying. You were my woman, my lover, and I didn't think of changing the context of our relationship…and I lost you. Then we met again and till yesterday I was struggling to get you to *talk* to me. I didn't think beyond getting you back."

Sarcasm huffed out of her. "You already planned our future liaison, following the same noncommittal pattern of our past one."

"Because when it comes to you, I'm not the long-term businessman but a beggar who can't hope enough to plan ahead. I felt I'd be lucky if I even got you to agree to that much. All I knew was that if we got together again, I wanted to be together always. So yes, I would have wanted marriage. Adam just accelerated the process. He's not the reason I'm proposing, he only gave me the reason to do it now."

Disbelief still blared from her eyes.

"I *can* legitimize Adam without marrying you, Lujayn."

A wave of bristling hurt rose off her, buffeted him. "Then by all means, go ahead."

He wanted to whack himself upside the head. Would he ever learn to not stoke her insecurity and poke her scars? "I'm only trying to prove to you I want to marry you only for you."

Cagey as an aggravated tigress, she said, "How would you legitimize him without marrying me?"

"I would say we were briefly married when he was conceived, an *orphy* secret marriage, or even a regular one, that ended in divorce. It would only take your corroboration, a few retroactive documents and he'd be my lawful son and heir."

She nodded, slowly, watchfully. "I'll corroborate anything that will be best for him."

He gauged the moment when she'd let him approach again, then reached for her. "I only want you to grant me the blessing of becoming my wife."

He felt her internal struggle, unable to let belief take hold after so many years of letdowns. "Is it my family's discovered rank that makes it possible for you to consider me for a wife now?"

He almost doubled over with the pain. Hers. What *he'd* inflicted when he'd made her feel she'd meant nothing to him.

"Let me make this unequivocally clear," he said, barely curbing the tremor in his voice. "I am proposing to *you*. If your family were criminals or worse, I would still propose to you. The woman who's been responsible for my life's most intense happiness and heartache. The only woman I've always and will always love."

Tears gushed from her eyes as if under pressure, her whole face crumpling under the onslaught of emotions too brutal to bear. "Don't...don't say what you don't mean...."

He cupped her face, hands trembling to the same frequency of her anguish. "It's another crime, my biggest one, that I never told you how much I mean it. I love you so much I was yours from the first moment I laid eyes on you." She hiccuped, her eyes enormous, her body shaking. "Even when I thought I'd lost you forever, when I told myself I should hate you, I couldn't be with anyone else. There *is* no one else for me."

And he saw it, the moment her barriers crumbled and belief flooded in, deluging her in its healing rush.

She surged into him, coming apart, burrowing into him, mashing her face into his chest, his neck, singeing his flesh with her tears, his name a litany on her lips. "Jalal...Jalal... oh, Jalal..."

"*Baba* Lal!"

They swung their heads as one at hearing Adam's voice.

He was running toward them with a smile showing off all his pearly teeth, his silver eyes crinkled with glee.

He threw himself at their legs, demanding to be picked up. They both bent, took him between their trembling bodies.

In between deluging his family in kisses, Jalal said, "I asked your Mama to marry me, *ya sugheeri*."

"Mama Lu!" Adam squeaked triumphantly.

Jalal chuckled, his heart expanding at the unbelievable blessing of having his family filling his arms. "That's what you've reduced us to? Lu and Lal? Sounds good to me."

Joy shone over her beloved face. "At first he likes to say things correctly, then goes on to interpret them to his liking."

"He can call me anything he likes."

"Oh, no, you're not making up for your absence from his life by letting him walk all over you and spoiling him." She pinched his cheek playfully. "You've been warned."

"And I'm duly chastised." He took her lips in a clinging kiss. "Adam is a wonderfully sunny and adjusted child, and I'll never sabotage your discipline. You show me the ropes until I put in the necessary time and effort to earn my role as his father."

"Easy for you to say now the sleepless nights are over."

He squashed her to him, and Adam in between them, who thought it was a game, squealed his enthusiasm. "Losing those months with you will remain a scar in my being, *ya rohi*. But I promise I'm never losing any more. I'll always be there for both of you till my dying day."

"It wasn't your fault you weren't there from the start. I…"

His lips silenced her agitation. "You never need to take responsibility for anything we lost. I wasn't there, didn't go with you to prenatal visits, didn't hold your hand during labor, didn't shoulder my share and yours of every second since when you needed me to. So you'll let me carry this." She gave a difficult nod. He quirked his lips, desperate to lighten the moment. "And though I escaped the sleepless nights, I'll now attend the toilet-training drama from the start."

She burst out laughing, a desperate edge to the brittle mirth, sounding relieved to leave this behind. "And secreting the keys to locked apartments, playing hide-and-seek with turned-off cell phones and eating breakfast from our golden retriever's bowl."

He looked in mock sternness at Adam. "Is that right, *ya sugheeri?*" Adam smiled unrepentantly and he sighed dramatically. "Seems I have my work cut out for me." He met her eyes, delighting in seeing the openness of emotion there at last. "But you realize you only soaked my shirt but didn't actually say yes?"

She flung her arms around him, squeezed him with all her strength, Adam and all. "A million yeses! A trillion!"

He shuddered in her arms, his lips roaming in prayer and gratitude over her and Adam's faces. "One will do, *ya hayati*. An irreversible one, my life."

Since Lujayn was twelve, she'd lost all those she'd loved.

Her mother and siblings to years of separation, her father to the pursuit of jobs that never lasted, Jalal to the gulf that had never let her have him in the first place, and Patrick to the end she'd known would take him away from their first day together.

Even when she'd managed to rescue her mother and father, she hadn't really had them back. The years apart had taken their toll and they weren't the people she remembered. Her siblings had barely reentered her life, with her brother mainly gone from all of theirs. Then she'd discovered her pregnancy, had suffocated with fear that she'd lose her baby, too. Adam had been born perfect and she'd still suffered panic attacks daily.

She'd hidden her turmoil, for Adam's sake, for her fragile family's. But inside, she'd come apart, expended all her energy to look intact. Then Jalal had reentered her life.

Her ferocious resistance hadn't been fueled by anger, but by fear. Fear of succumbing only to find him a mirage again.

But if she could believe the past twenty-four hours, he wasn't only real, he was forever.

Surely nothing could be so perfect. She couldn't really have the completeness of Jalal and his love, the transcendent joy of their united family. Could she?

But he pledged she could have anything she dreamed of. He swore that she not only had him, but had always had him.

And here she was, in the middle of their family room, in the villa he'd bought by a phone call the moment she'd said she loved it, watching him and their son playing and talking and laughing as if they always had.

When Jalal anxiously had inquired about her silence, she'd said she was luxuriating in watching him and Adam together. From then on, he'd stopped worrying and let her indulge her every starving sense and unborn hope in the wonder and beauty of her man and her son forging a life-long bond.

Dahab came back at night and took a sleeping Adam with her to the hotel, where she told her family they'd all stay the night. She'd cooked up this plan when Jalal had announced his proposal and Lujayn's hard-won acceptance. After going ballistic, especially with the prospect of preparing a royal wedding, Dahab thought the newly engaged couple needed a night together, before wedding preparations drove them crazy and apart for the duration.

Though all Lujayn wanted the moment they reentered the villa was to tear Jalal out of his clothes and lose her mind all over him, he had other plans.

He wasn't gulping her down like he had last night, not even if she begged. And how she did. Tonight, he was woo-ing her, sealing their pact of forever with affection and har-mony before moving on to abandon and ecstasy. In short, he drove her insane.

For the next hours till midnight, he and Labeeb—who now answered her every word with "my eyes to you"—collaborated in waiting on her, cooking for her, serving her and just all around spoiling her.

She'd endured it all, reliving every sensation of Jalal's possession. It all blossomed inside her mind and body, a memory replaying the glide of his flesh on and inside hers, the harshness of his desire biting into it, filling her body, his voice filling her ears, his breath filling her lungs, his taste her mouth. She'd sat there trying not to squirm with rising arousal and was immensely relieved when Labeeb finally disappeared.

Jalal, who'd watched her with knowing indulgence, his eyes promising her the satisfaction of her every hunger, now rose, came around to her. He took her to the middle of the floor, drew her into a gentle yet possessive embrace, danced with her to the thrilling beauty of a dreamy Azmaharian piece.

She laid her head on his chest, swaying to the tempo of his steady heart, her own stampeding, her lips and nipples stinging, every nerve discharging....

"Now to abandon and ecstasy."

His bass voice caressed her ear, had her core contracting, her toes curling. He'd almost driven her over the edge with just a declaration. Knowing how devastatingly he carried out his promises was enough to unleash the full force of her arousal.

She erupted in his arms, dragged him behind her to the bedroom suite. Theirs now.... She closed the double doors, leaned on them.

"I want you to do something for me."

His mirth evaporated at her husky words, his face settling into the stark lines of passion—fierce and resolute. "Anything. And everything. Always. Just ask."

"Let me have my way with you. *All* the way."

The flare of sensual savagery in his eyes seared through her already-inflamed flesh until she felt like one exposed nerve.

"Then have it. Any and every way you crave."

He started undressing as he talked. Her first reaction was to cry out for him to let her do it. But she held back, let him perform that mind-melting striptease for her, watching and burning, her muscles buzzing with the effort not to charge him. Soon, she placated herself. Now, she got to revel in the beauty she'd thought she'd live deprived of.

The night Adam had been conceived and last night had been too mindless and short-lived. She hadn't had the chance to savor his magnificence. And even this description was an understatement. Time had conspired to turn what she'd thought was virile perfection into something that defied description, even belief.

Burnished bronze skin overlay heavy yet lithe muscles, sculpted from power and symmetry. Broad shoulders flowed into defined chest and abdomen, narrow hips and taut buttocks, dominant thighs and muscled legs, every inch chiseled from maleness and stamina. She knew from experience that even his toes were beautiful. He was a work of divine art down to his pores.

Then he stepped out of his briefs.

Letting her get only a glimpse of what she'd soon, please soon, impale herself on, he turned, simmered an inviting look over his shoulder and sauntered like a smug feline to the bed.

In languorous movements, he propped his great body against the headboard, stretched out his long limbs, his erection hard and long, heavy and thick, ready for her to come ride it.

Feeling that nip of familiar intimidation, she tore things in her haste to get rid of her clothes. She didn't care. Any slower and she would incinerate them right off, anyway.

Then she bolted for him.

She crawled over him, worshipping him from legs to lips. By the time she straddled his hips, he'd given up any pretense at deliberateness and was panting as heavily as she was, his groans as pained as hers, his hands roaming her in a fever, his body matching her own shudders.

He still didn't hurry her, didn't drag her over him and thrust inside her to end their suffering, letting her set the pace. But she only wanted to hurtle through this first joining. So she did.

Digging her hands into his shoulders, crashing her lips down on his, drinking deep of his taste, she bore down, taking him all the way to her womb in one downward stroke.

Agony and ecstasy ripped her apart. The unforgettable, almost unbearable expansion his size forged inside her had her thrashing over him, withdrawing to escape the shredding pain, plunging back to gorge on the maddening pleasure. She was molten yet his girth almost didn't fit. And still it fit to such levels of perfection, the carnality, the reality of feeling him like that again, now when love had been declared, had her weeping. He licked her tears, growling her name, igniting her fire higher, driving her harder, until she burst into the flames of a devastating completion.

Shock waves expanded, collapsed, then again, milking his hard flesh of every pleasure, for her and for him. She shrieked his name as the detonations of each orgasm severed all her nerves, as his seed shot inside her in one scalding surge after another, bathing her intimate flesh, filling her womb, fulfilling her....

From the depths of boneless bliss, she felt his hands stroking awareness into her satiated body. She was sprawled over him, her flesh still fluttering with aftershocks around him as he remained buried inside her.

A lion's purr rumbled beneath her ear. "I need you to promise me you'll frequently override my Neanderthal tendencies to dominate you and just have your way with me like that."

Her lips spread lazily. "You got it. Very frequently."

His chuckle changed into a groan as her inner flesh spasmed over his intact hardness. "Forget what I just said.

The need to go all caveman over you is becoming unstoppable."

She giggled as he heaved up, swung her beneath him and pressed her between the mattress and his hot, hard bulk.

A long time after he'd devastated her, he brought her over him again and sighed in contentment. "You feel...different."

Euphoria screeched to a halt. "Not as tight as before?"

"No." All bliss drained away as she wriggled, severing their union. He caught her, turned her on her back, rose above her. "I mean it's *not* that. Physically, you're the same, or it might be a bit less of a struggle to fit inside you. You just *feel* different."

Still unsure, still worried, she probed, "Because of Adam?"

"Because of *us*. *You're* different. *I* am. We've matured. We're certain we want each other, no substitutes. It makes us better at this." His lips quirked. "Though you must stop improving right here. Any better and I might expire."

Flooded with relief, hoping she'd soon stop having those attacks of uncertainty, she looked up at him adoringly. "Do you know you have the most beautiful eyes in existence? If we have a girl, I hope she'll have your eyes."

He stilled. "You want more children?"

Every uncertainty crashed down on her again. She swallowed. "I'm just saying, if one day you think we should..."

He interrupted her agitation. "I think we should have as many children as you're willing to have. I want anything you want, whenever you want it."

Wobbling with yo-yoing anxiety and relief, her hand trembled as she smoothed it down his stubbled cheek. "Then I want to binge on you without interruptions a bit longer before we embark on our next miracle."

"Then binge away." His grin was delight itself as he swept her up in his arms and took her to the bathroom.

* * *

The rest of the night, followed by next day, were spent in a blur of lovemaking.

By evening, they reluctantly considered the rest of the world, called her family back to the villa and announced their news.

They'd agreed on a story. They met after Patrick died, sought solace in each other, got married. But she thought she'd made a mistake, insisted on a divorce. He'd been trying to get her back ever since. He'd told her it wasn't far from the truth.

Her family's reaction was one of dazed delight. And they were even more stunned, along with Lujayn, when Jalal announced they'd get married a week from now. He'd assured them it would be enough time to prepare a wedding worthy of Lujayn.

Carried on the wave of collective happiness and enthusiasm, Lujayn spent the next day at the royal palace where Jalal had decided to have the wedding. He gave her and her family, foremost Dahab, free rein to set the place up for a legendary wedding. Lujayn didn't want any of that, but he insisted he wanted to give her this, and to please humor him.

Spiraling deeper than ever in love with him, she accepted this as another of his efforts to make up for the years they'd lost, and the unintentional pain and alienation he'd inflicted on her. Though she didn't need any tributes or any amends, she knew *he* needed to make them. She'd always give him everything he needed.

She'd just left her family and Adam in the *Qobba* hall, literally the Dome, the name coming from its residing under the palace's central, hundred-foot mosaic one. She had to find Jalal, get his opinion about the seating plan for his personal friends.

Entering the antechamber to the royal office on the first floor, she heard a voice that wasn't his.

If voices could have colors, that one would be pitch-black. "...already behaving as if you own the place."

She heard Jalal exhale. "And it's great to see you again, too, Rashid."

That had to be Rashid Aal Munsoori, the third candidate for the throne. She knew he was a distant maternal relative of Jalal's, and a once-best friend. She had no idea how things stood between them now, especially with being rivals for the throne.

From what she'd heard so far, it didn't sound like they were on particularly friendly terms. At least, from Rashid's side. He was more or less accusing Jalal of usurping the palace as his own.

But Jalal wasn't abusing his power, had paid a major sum to the kingdom's treasury to use the palace for their wedding. She'd said they could have rented the Taj Mahal for a month for that amount. He'd countered they could have used the royal palace of Zohayd for free, which was better than both places. In fact, King Amjad, his oldest brother, had snarked his head off, telling him to skip along and have a rehearsal wedding in his motherland to please his in-laws, then come have an actual one in his *father*land, in a palace *really* worthy of his wife and heir.

But Jalal considered he was hitting two birds with one stone having their wedding here. Giving her a wedding in *her* motherland, reinforcing her family's status and pumping money into the kingdom without it looking like a charitable donation.

She chewed her lip as she debated if she should wait until Rashid left, or leave and return when he had.

Her intimate flesh quivered at contemplating the long walk to and from the *Qobba* hall. Though the soreness she'd begged Jalal to inflict on her was delicious, it did make walking straight quite a feat. She didn't want to give everyone *too* clear an indication how they'd spent the time since their reunion. Now that Azmahar would feature heavily in their future, she had to get used to observing the land's conservative tendencies.

Deciding to wait, she picked one of the Arabic books in the mini-library in the antechamber. Might as well brush up on her Arabic reading skills as she waited.

She started reading then everything inside her froze as something Rashid was saying made her listen.

"…after Haidar thwarted your plans to use Roxanne to gain the upper hand in the campaign, you think giving the fairy-tale-addicted Azmaharians a sob story about restored honor, estranged spouses and a secret male heir will sway them in your favor?"

Her heart choked on its beats waiting for Jalal's answer. He would hit Rashid's venom back with as much conviction.

But he didn't. He didn't answer at all.

She couldn't even fathom his reaction from the quality of his silence. How was he looking at Rashid? Ridiculing? Exasperated?

Rashid was talking again. "Go ahead, shackle yourself with a woman and a child you don't want in your desperate bid for the throne. It will be a fitting punishment for you to be literally left holding the baby with not as much as a cabinet seat to collapse in defeat on."

She was shaking from head to toe when Jalal finally talked.

"Haidar told me how you had changed. I thought he was exaggerating. Turns out he's been his usual reticent self and left out the juicy parts. What happened to you, Rashid?"

A long, nerve-racking silence followed.

Then in a voice as still as the grave, Rashid said, "Didn't you just say your distorted mirror image told you?"

"He only told me the end result, not the process. We know nothing about you beyond the time when you joined the army and kept drifting farther and farther away until you disappeared on us totally. And then—" she could almost see Jalal's frustrated gesture in the beat of silence "—*this* came back in your stead."

"*This* is the real me." Rashid's voice remained expressionless, and more hair-raising for it. "The only me you'll ever see again. So if either of you deficient hybrids thinks you have a prayer against me, spare yourself the indignity. You in particular are so pathetic I decided to show you the mercy of advising you not to sacrifice your freedom at the altar of the kingly ambitions that you are destined to never fulfill."

Lujayn stood rooted as Rashid's voice approached and as he opened the ajar office door. He saw her immediately, stopped.

He stared back at her, a force of darkness in male form. And that scar…

She would have lurched if she wasn't frozen, inside and out.

Then he exhaled. "I'm sorry you had to hear that, Sheikha Lujayn. At least now you can make an informed decision."

He bowed deferentially as he passed her even as Jalal's shouted curse penetrated her numbness.

Jalal charged into the antechamber, aggravation blazing at Rashid's receding back, morphing into anxiety as his eyes fell on her.

Before he could say anything, she whispered, "Is this why you want us, Jalal?"

His face twisted as if she'd stabbed him. "You still think that badly of me, Lujayn? You mistrust me that deeply?"

She swallowed, shook her head. She trusted him, but…

He took her shoulders in trembling hands. "Rashid was just messing with me, like he's been messing with Haidar since he's come back to Azmahar. Beside whatever has turned him against us personally, he considers us interlopers, more Zohaydan than Azmaharians. He's employing psychological warfare to get us out of the way. But you must know everything you heard him say has no basis in fact. I want you, and Adam, for one reason only. Because I can't live without you. Tell me you believe me, *ya habibati!*"

She threw herself at him, clung as if she'd escaped certain death. "I do, oh, God, Jalal, I do."

He groaned against her cheek, her lips. "I can't bear it if you have any doubts, *ya'yooni.* I'll withdraw my candidacy."

"No!" She pulled away so he could read her urgency, conviction in her eyes. "Don't even think it! I just love you so much, am so happy, it's making me jittery and unable to believe my luck."

He pulled her once again into his embrace, agitation draining, indulgence flooding back. "It isn't luck, it's the least you deserve. And whether I become king or not doesn't matter. I only want to love you and Adam and live to make you happier still."

As she lost herself in his kiss, his safety and promise, something still told her there was no way life would let her have all that and not eventually interfere....

Eleven

The tables' accents and the color of bridesmaids' dresses had just been decided. *Dahabi.* As the "golden" girl, Dahab herself had decreed the color was a no-brainer.

What remained was everything else. The flower arrangements, the grounds' ornaments and lighting, the hall decorations, the catering menu. The *kooshah*—where Lujayn and Jalal would preside over the festivities—was a matter of particular contention. And Lujayn didn't even want to think what would happen when she had to give a final word on her dress. Not to mention accessories. Everyone had an opinion, and of course, it was the right one.

She'd been stunned when her mother had come passionately to life the moment Jalal had set the wedding date, becoming a whirlwind of organizing and decision-making. More stunning was her aunt's all-out enthusiasm. She'd been recovering from her mastectomy at breathtaking speed, especially after knowing she wouldn't need chemo or radiation. But Lujayn bet her mother's and aunt's soaring spirits had most to do with their restored social status, and Jalal treating them like queens. They almost grew wings every time he walked in, kissing their hands and calling them *hamati* and *hamati el tanyah*—my mother-in-law and second mother-in-law.

But he'd done way more. He'd turned the palace into a workshop for them. He had tailors, jewelers, chefs, florists and workmen from just about every trade at their beck and call to put together every detail of the wedding. Her womenfolk were getting more delirious by the second, feeling like they'd fallen into a wonderland where they'd fulfill every feminine fantasy. Dahab had told him he'd firmly earned the title of genie.

After the first day, when she'd realized the scope of the details, Lujayn had thought they'd have to postpone the wedding. Jalal wouldn't hear of it. His rationalization? If they gave her womenfolk a year, they'd still come up with more details. Though she agreed, she couldn't get around the slowing down that working in shifts caused so someone would always be with Adam. Jalal, always ready with a solution, had whisked Adam away till the wedding.

She'd smothered him in kisses. Not because he'd taken Adam off her hands, but because of the eagerness with which he had. She'd also pinched his luscious butt for maneuvering her into giving him this opening to have Adam all to himself. He'd pinched hers right back, telling her to get to work, triumphantly informing Adam that, as men, their part in that legendary wedding would consist of jumping into their costumes and showing up.

He'd been bringing Adam to visit twice a day. Adam considered the preparations a huge game park and Jalal let him play among them to his heart's content, watching him like a hawk all the while. During their last visit hours ago, her family had wanted to drag her to more dress fittings, had shooed Jalal away so he wouldn't accidentally see the dress they might decide on.

She'd insisted on seeing him and Adam out, silently begging him to support her decision. She'd needed a breather from the single-mindedness of her bridesmaid-zillas. When they'd protested they'd only checked off six items from a list of fourteen today, couldn't afford a break, he'd come to her rescue, asserting he needed a kiss, one not for her family's eyes.

Cheeks blazing and eyes gleaming, they'd let her escape.

Not that he'd let her escape *him*. After he'd given Adam to Labeeb, he'd dragged her into one of the palace's secret rooms, taken her, hard and fast and almost blew her mind.

She'd gone back to her family in a stupor and had gone along with anything anyone had said ever since. Hence all that gold that would turn the *Qobba* hall into a replica of Midas's vault.

But then Qusr Al Majd—literally Palace of Glory—would give said vault, and all tourist-attraction palaces in the world a run for their money. It might not be as majestic as Zohayd's royal palace, but it was surely striking, and like Haidar had said, felt like some elaborate beast from a Dungeons & Dragons fantasy.

Haidar had come yesterday to meet his twin's "best-kept secret" and thank her for proving his "wolf" theory about Jalal right. Jalal had teased his twin back saying one of the things *he* thanked her for was making him beat Haidar to something—having a "cub" first. Haidar had volleyed that he'd beat him again. Roxanne was pregnant with another set of Aal Shalaan twins!

She'd liked Haidar on sight, was so grateful that he and Jalal had patched up their lifelong differences. She knew she'd grow to love him and, if possible, that had intensified her happiness.

She now sat ensconced on a window seat in the meeting-room-turned-workshop, her outline still blurred from Jalal's lovemaking, dreamily watching Azmahar's autumn sun setting, and its velvety, star-studded night taking over.

"So this was why you've been avoiding me!"

Lujayn started, burning in instant embarrassment. Aliyah!

She jumped down from the seat, turned to the woman who'd once been her lifeline, her heart quivering with delight to see her again. And she almost gasped.

Aliyah had always been beautiful, but now…now she was glorious. What fairy-tale queens should look like.

As tall as Lujayn but slimmer—at least now *she* was full of "lethal curves" as Jalal insisted—Aliyah had the bearing of a woman who'd long borne the weight of position and power. Having two children had only deepened her tranquility, and having the certainty of a great man's love had crystallized her femininity.

Aliyah had another gorgeous woman with her who looked as if her body and spirit had been spun from fire. Roxanne Gleeson, now known as Haidar's wife, Princess Roxanne Aal Shalaan—a woman she'd once thought had been one of Jalal's lovers.

He'd explained away the misconception that had long torn at her, telling her that Roxanne had actually been like the sister he'd longed to have in his all-male family. According to Jalal, Aliyah had been revealed to be his sister in time to get married and hoarded by that possessive jackass of a husband.

When she'd giggled that Aliyah sure didn't agree with his opinion of King Kamal of Judar, he'd harrumphed. Kamal, and he, *were* confirmed jackasses. They'd just lucked into having phenomenal women love them. Just like Haidar had with Roxanne. Thankfully, after long years of estrangement, Roxanne had become his sister at last, Haidar's wife and an Aal Shalaan princess.

Before Lujayn could do more than kiss the two women, her womenfolk came swarming. Queen Aliyah of Judar was one of the two big-deal queens in the region, the other being Queen Maram of Zohayd, King Amjad's wife and Lujayn's almost sister-in-law. Roxanne had also made a big splash in Azmahar on two fronts, first as the kingdom's foremost politico-financial analyst, and now as Haidar's wife.

Soon, the two women joined their dress-choosing ritual with utmost enthusiasm. For the next couple hours, Lujayn felt like a doll, being put into and pulled out of dresses that she then had to model, walk, sit, run, dance and climb stairs in, with the ladies scribbling down comments and ratings for each, then discussing pros and cons spiritedly.

Aliyah finally insisted Lujayn try on a dress, to everyone's surprise. It was fashioned from an incredible amalgam of tulle, taffeta and lace, worked in breathtaking arabesque patterns of sequins, mirrors, pearls and silk thread. A strapless, hugging bodice would accentuate Lujayn's breasts and waist and a skirt lush in layers, yet not flaring, would showcase her curves. In short, perfect.

But their unanimous objection to it? It was *gray*.

Aliyah laughingly reminded them they were talking to the woman who'd rocked the region wearing black for her wedding. And then it *wasn't gray*. It was silvered dawn and deepening twilight and every shade in between. And it looked as if it was spun from the threads of Lujayn's own unique colors.

They all deferred to Aliyah's opinion, not as queen, but as the world-renowned artist among them.

Lujayn still felt their skepticism, until the moment they saw it on her. And they all shouted simultaneously, "That's it!"

It was only then that Aliyah revealed that her vision for the whole scene was now complete. With the bridesmaids and matrons of honor all golden, with her coloring and dress, Lujayn would stand out like a black-and-white silver-screen moon goddess.

Another hour passed before Lujayn was finally allowed to take off the dress, after picking a *tarhah*—a veil—for it. Aliyah and Roxanne both promised to bring her just the pieces to go with that outfit from the royal jewels of Judar and Zohayd.

Leaving her family boggling over that prospect, Aliyah and Roxanne spirited Lujayn away for a much-needed break.

In the blessed silence and isolation of a sitting room at the farthest end of the palace, she finally grinned at them. "Thanks for the rescue, ladies. It's a good thing weddings are a once-in-a-lifetime thing. I don't think I'd survive that again."

"Don't worry, you won't need to." Roxanne beamed, looking the image of glowing health in her early second trimester. "You're marrying an Aal Shalaan. Those are for-life catches."

"And Aal Masoods," Aliyah piped in.

Lujayn's smile widened, remembering Jalal's jackass comment concerning Aliyah's Aal Masood husband. No way was she telling Aliyah and have her kick Jalal's luscious behind for it.

Roxanne sighed. "We're all Aal Shalaan princesses now, whether by birth or marriage. And let me tell you, Lujayn, from, uh…intensive experience, there's *nothing* better."

Lujayn nodded vigorously, still tingling from her own recent "intensive experience" with her Aal Shalaan prince.

"Did you notice how my own messed-up origins make me related to everyone in some way or another?" Aliyah asked.

Lujayn grinned. "Yep, you're the only one who grew up a Morgan, turned out to be an Aal Shalaan and then became an Aal Masood, too."

"While I once felt it was a mess I'd never survive, it proved to be the best blessing possible." Aliyah winked at Lujayn. "Finding out you're not who you thought you were is turning out fantastic for you, too, isn't it? Not to mention catching the heart of one of those forever guys." Aliyah's dark eyes sparked gold, reflecting the sun streaks in her mahogany hair. "And though you kept everyone in the dark, I can't believe you had *me* fooled. You missed your vocation as an actress, lady."

Lujayn fidgeted under Aliyah's teasing scrutiny. "Yeah, well, it wasn't something I could share at the time. I've long stopped being a model, too. I entered college when I married Patrick, got a degree in economics and business management. I'm preparing a master's degree now."

"Wow, I can't believe just how much we have in common!" Roxanne exclaimed. "Having you in the family is going to be even more fun than I anticipated. And you must make use of me if you ever need any help with your projects and assets. I'm a decent financial adviser, I'm told."

"They're not mine," Lujayn said, then explained the situation with Patrick's family. "I only controlled everything until we made sure they were out of the way. I'll soon turn it over to the charities and concerns he'd specified. Any money or shares my family got was payment for our work, so I'm not the billionaire heiress everybody thinks I am. I just never refuted it since I was still wrapping things up before I came back to Azmahar."

Roxanne looked impressed. "And that you managed to keep that from someone like me tells me everything about how good you are at what you do. I've heard there are many concerns vying to do business with you as Patrick's heiress. Prepare for the restoration of some serious personal space when the news comes out."

Roxanne's words suddenly hit her with a realization.

She never really explained to Jalal how things stood.

But he had once made it clear he believed she possessed Patrick's wealth. What if part of her...acceptability now was because of her assumed wealth? Princes did have far more to consider in marriage than normal men. Money and power married money and power. What if, when he realized she didn't have either, it changed everything?

From then on, she barely knew what Aliyah or Roxanne said or what she answered. At some point they stood up, kissed her, and promising to join her wedding preparation mayhem starting tomorrow, they took their leave.

In a similar fugue, she returned to her family who tossed her around in more wedding details before they called it a night. Instead of spending the night in the palace like them, she slipped away to Jalal's villa. Or as he insisted it now was, home.

Labeeb received her at the gates and suggested that she surprise Jalal. He had turned out to be a closet romantic. Before he disappeared, he reassured her that Adam was asleep after a bath that had left him happily exhausted and Jalal and Labeeb wet. Both grown-ups had their baby monitors on their person, but there hadn't been a peep from Adam for the past three hours.

Inside the villa, Jalal's favorite music, a hybrid of western, Zohaydan and Azmharian, was emanating from their family room, wrapping her in its evocative magic. Approaching in silence, she stood watching Jalal as he sat on the couch in profile. He was covered in a laptop and open files, looking totally engrossed, and more heartbreakingly beautiful than ever. Barefoot, hair tousled, black trainers riding low on his hips, and the rest of his body was exposed to her devouring.

Seeing him this way, relaxed in their home, surged in her heart with thankfulness and longing. But anxiety ruled all other emotions.

He turned suddenly, his gaze slamming into hers, delight flaring in his eyes.

After hurriedly clearing his lap, he jumped up to his feet and rushed to her, arms open. He swept her off the floor, groaned into her hair, *"Habibati..."* before he took her lips, submerged her in his hunger.

When he let her draw a breath, her feet almost buckled as he put her back on them.

"So how did you do it?"

She blinked.

He elaborated. "Escape your posse of wedding wardens?"

She hugged him, filled with the wonder of him in her arms. "I slipped out behind their backs, how else?"

"They intimidated me so much with their lists and color schemes I didn't even dare ask you to do this."

She chuckled at the incongruous image he painted, the desert warrior tiptoeing around a bunch of females in fear they'd attack him with ribbons and cake tastings.

His laughter echoed hers as gravity relinquished its hold over her, delivered her into his power. She plunged into his craving, wanting to take all she could now, before anything happened to spoil this magic, as she lived in fear it would....

The night's breeze was blowing their bedroom's gauzy, cream-colored curtains in a hypnotic dance when she finally resurfaced from another surrender to ecstasy in his arms. He was stroking her sweat-drenched, still-quivering body when without preamble she poured out everything about Patrick's assets.

He kept on caressing her throughout her account.

When she fell silent, he shrugged. "And?"

She rose over him, anxious to read his expression. There was only his usual indulgence. "*And* I'm not an heiress."

"Darn." He combed his fingers through her tousled tresses, his grin devilish. "I was hoping you'd lend me a billion or two to develop a cloaking device so I can make love to you anywhere."

"Be serious for a second here, okay?" she groaned.

His eyes sobered. "What's to be serious about? Your involvement or lack of in Patrick's legacy doesn't change my pledge to fulfill it. Other than that, what does your being an heiress or not matter?" He rose on his elbows, frowning. "You still think anything but you matters to me?"

Her gaze wavered under the disappointment in his. "I—I just wondered…y'know, with you being a prince, if—if…"

She groaned again, words trailing off.

He heaved up, had her rolling to her side to watch him stride from the bed to the desk by the veranda. He picked up an MP3 player, tapped the screen and walked back with it held up to his lips.

"I, Jalal Aal Shalaan, hereby solemnly swear, on my life, on my honor, on my son—whose finger alone I value above my life—that one woman has ever and will ever be the largest part of my soul, just because she is who she is. My cherished, beloved Lujayn."

Reaching the bed again, he held the player down to her. It replayed the pledge he'd just recorded.

"Whenever you have any worries and I'm not around, play this." With a teary sob, she launched herself at him,

raining laughter and tears all over him. "And when I am
just let me know, and I'll take care of it for you, like this...."

And for the rest of the night, he showed her how he'd always take care of her every worry and need....

The day was here.

The day he'd tell the whole world he was Lujayn's. The
day he'd start his lifelong mission to heal all the injuries and
injustice that he and his family had dealt her.

His gaze panned over his surroundings, and his lips
spread. He had to give credit to Lujayn's womenfolk. They
had pulled off a miracle. He'd teased them, wondering if
they did have a genie at their command. They had turned
the neglected palace with its hideously ornate interiors, and
especially the *Qobba* hall, into a most tasteful and lavish
setting from an *Arabian Nights* fable. A setting worthy of
his princess, the love of his life and the mother of his incomparable son.

His family, who had all arrived that morning, were now
sitting in the huge semicircle facing the *kooshah* where he
and Lujayn would join the *ma'zoon* to scribe their marriage
vows in the book of matrimony. His father hadn't looked
this well and happy in...ever. His marriage to Anna Beaumont, Aliyah's biological mother, and the love of *his* life
was doing him wonders. After a lifetime wasted in two mar-
riages, first to the mother of Amjad, Harres and Shaheen
followed by the harsher blow of his and Haidar's mother,
their father deserved a break. And he'd at last gotten it. Anna
seemed to be formed of pure love for her husband. His father had earned all this beauty and devotion, had done the
right thing in abdicating the throne of Zohayd to Amjad.
Now he could enjoy what was left of his life with the one
woman his heart had chosen, and whom life and duty had
deprived him of for three decades.

But though he was delighted for his father, tonight he could tell him and his older brothers and Haidar, that they could move over and vacate the position of happiest man on earth.

A sigh of pleasure and anticipation escaped him, as Lujayn's favorite jasmine scent filled the gigantic hall, carried on a dreamlike mist.

Adam whooped and jumped in his arms. Heart pounding, his gaze moved to where Adam's tiny finger was excitedly pointing. Lujayn's bridal procession had just entered the hall, preceded by Dahab.

They looked like walking jewelry with their golden dresses. Every female in Lujayn's family had joined the ranks. Almost all in his had. His brothers' wives were all there, Johara, Talia, Maram and Roxanne. Aliyah was walking with her daughter, who skipped beside her looking like a pixie, and actually completing the image by throwing golden dust behind her.

The only women who didn't make it to this wedding was Laylah, one of the three precious female Aal Shalaans. And his mother.

No one even spoke of Sondoss, as if her mention would be the evil spell that would spoil everything. He couldn't blame them. Though he visited her whenever he could, he sure wasn't inviting her into his life now that it revolved around Lujayn and Adam. The farther she stayed from Lujayn and her family, the better.

The heavy, driving beat of the *zaffah* started, the region's traditional bridal procession rhythm. After a percussive intro, with Dahab acting as cheerleader, the whole attendance started singing the most famous regional bridal song, chanting the praises of the bride, congratulating her on her dashing groom and wishing her bountiful happiness and blessed progeny.

Every nerve strained for Lujayn's entrance as Adam's excitement reached fever pitch and he starting yelling her name. The song was repeated twice as the bridal procession took their places, surrounding the *kooshah* in petal-like patterns, and everyone pinned their gazes on the hall's entrance.

The entrance remained empty. The song was repeated three times more, and it remained so. After the fifth repetition the music stopped. Murmurs rose, then spread like wildfire. Everybody was looking around, expecting some surprise. When none came, they turned their gazes to him. He stood there, frozen, unable to think. He felt nothing but Adam wriggling in his arms. He put Adam down and he ran to his grandmother. Jalal met her gaze and saw in her bewilderment that she had no idea what was going on. And that she was growing more anxious with every heartbeat.

"You wait right here. We'll go find out what's going on," Harres said, who'd come back from talking to the *ma'zoon*.

"What *could* be going on?" Haidar asked, who'd been standing beside him. As his closest brothers, both would be the marriage witnesses. "She either changed her mind about the dress, or she's keeping you waiting a bit to punish you for all the years you didn't even think of marrying her."

Haidar gave him a reassuring backslap and strode away.

Jalal stood there, his mind stalled. Nothing would restart it but the sight of Lujayn.

Time warped, everything grated. The air, the weight of his costume, people's glances.

Then Haidar and Harres strode into the hall again.

Harres swerved, headed for Amjad, Shaheen and their father. Haidar walked up to him.

Jalal could only stare at Haidar as he stopped before him.

He couldn't read his expression. Wouldn't. Everything

refused to cooperate. Wouldn't work. His mind. His voice. His heart.

Then with his voice as dark and regretful as his expression, Haidar said, "Lujayn is gone."

Twelve

*G*one.

The word revolved in his head again and again. It made no sense. It was impossible. Untrue.

Lujayn couldn't be gone.

Then a chain reaction started, sparked by an insupportable thought. The only way she could be gone.

She'd been taken. *Kidnapped.*

His mind overflowed with dread. Talons of desperation pierced his brain as his fingers sank into the one thing left in his world, his twin's immovable support. His vision phased in and out as a voice, rabid with fear, barely recognized as his, formed no words, just her name, over and over. He couldn't say anything else and make it real.

Haidar's words cleaved inside his skull. "Go to pieces later, Jalal. We need to say something to this crowd, contain this catastrophe first, then we're getting you out of here and…"

He pushed Haidar away, unable to bear any more talk and ran out of the hall, a storm of agitation exploding all around him. He heard cries, inquiries, exclamations that pummeled him with their alarm. He pushed through the hindering bodies and presences. If he ran hard enough, he might still find her, save her....

Inexorable forces pulled him back. He turned and found Haidar and Harres holding on to him. Amjad and Shaheen were running toward them.

"Where do you think you're going?" Haidar hissed.

"I won't even say I can imagine how you feel," Harres said. "Because I damn well can't. But let's slow down for a moment...."

"Slow down?" Jalal roared. "Lujayn has been kidnapped and you want me to slow down?"

"Kidnapped?" Shaheen frowned, looking among his brothers.

Amjad came to a stop a couple feet away. "So you think the only way she'd stand you up at the *ma'zoon* is if she'd been kidnapped?"

Jalal rounded on him snarling, shaking off Haidar's and Harres's shackles.

Amjad deflected his aggression with unperturbed sarcasm. "She wasn't kidnapped, so you can stop working on this heart attack."

Everything inside Jalal stopped, clamped down on only three words. *She wasn't kidnapped.*

Relief razed through him. "Are—are you sure?"

His brothers exchanged an uncomfortable look. Then, exhaling heavily, Haidar handed him a note.

There were only three words on it, too. In Lujayn's handwriting.

I'm sorry. Lujayn.

He stared at the words, as if they'd multiply, as if they'd

say more if he looked hard enough. The same three words remained. Explaining nothing.

"Where did you find this?" Jalal rasped.

Haidar exhaled again. "In the room where the ladies had left her, to have a moment to herself as she'd requested, before walking out to the bridal procession. She'd taken off her wedding dress and left through the balcony."

Jalal shook his head, discounting every word, every evidence. "That's impossible. She wouldn't leave. Not of her own accord. A note doesn't prove she wasn't kidnapped. She could have been forced to write it, to—to…" Moisture that felt like acid forced its way out of his eyes, slithered down his cheeks. "*Ya Ullah*…Lujayn…*ya Ullah*…"

Harres hugged him roughly around the shoulders. "She *hasn't* been kidnapped, Jalal, so stop going crazy, at least about this."

"Guards tried to stop her," Haidar said. "But she insisted they'd be punished if they detained her. They were so flustered by her intensity they let her go. By the time they informed Fadi and he checked the airport, she'd boarded a flight. He ordered them to stop takeoff and disembark her, but she invoked her American citizenship and they took off."

Jalal stared at Haidar, finding no more places to hide.

She was really gone.

But it couldn't be because she wanted to. She loved him. More than loved him. He was half of her soul as much as she was his. And the other half was Adam. She wouldn't leave either of them. She'd die without them. Just like they would without her.

Seemed he'd said that out loud, because Amjad was answering him. "She knows without marrying her, you won't be able to stop her family from taking Adam back to her. So she only left you."

He rounded on Amjad. "Would *you* believe Maram would ever leave you?"

Amjad's gaze lengthened at his vehemence. Then he shrugged. "Then Lujayn left but didn't really leave. *That* leaves one possibility."

Everyone turned to Amjad, all at a loss.

Amjad raised ridiculing eyebrows. "You really can't figure it out? What is this, a collective, selective blindness?"

Harres punched Amjad in the arm. "One more useless word, and king or not, the next punch puts you flat on your back."

Amjad rubbed his arm, gave Harres then Shaheen a pitying glance. "Those two—" he flicked a hand at Haidar and Jalal "—I can understand, having been genetically tampered with. But what's *your* excuse?" Shaheen joined Harres in a threatening step, and Amjad's palms on both their chests held them off as he shook his head derisively, let out a disgusted huff. "Sondoss, what else?"

Jalal's heart gave one sickeningly painful twist at hearing his mother's name. Then it all fell into place.

It *was* his mother. She was the one who'd made Lujayn leave.

"We warned you she wasn't through messing in your lives." Amjad scowled at him and Haidar. "But you went all filial on us and exiled her in that tropical resort instead of letting me devise a dungeon worthy of her dragon-ness. Now you pay the price."

"If you believe a dungeon would have ended her danger," Shaheen scoffed, "then you don't realize what Sondoss is."

Harres nodded. "Jalal and Haidar made the right decision, if for the wrong reasons. An imprisoned Sondoss would have been far more dangerous than an exiled one. The worst she's evidently done so far was sabotage a wedding. But had she been in prison, she would have plotted the end of the world to get out."

Amjad smirked. "Good boys. You're not as gullible as I sometimes fear. I'll keep you as my heir and spare." He quirked an eyebrow at all of them. "But it took us years to accidentally stumble on her diabolical plot. Want to bet that in due course, we'll discover she's put far worse in motion than spoiling a wedding? Maybe even that world's end scenario?" He panned his gaze to Jalal. "Though from looking at you, she might have ended yours."

Shaheen glared at Amjad. "There might still be another explanation to all this."

Haidar shook his head, looking as shaken as Jalal felt. "No. Mother makes a perfect one."

Harres nodded. "Agreed. One thing I can't figure out, though. How did she get Lujayn to leave?"

Jalal turned, walked away. His brothers let him go this time.

He didn't know how. But he would find out.

He would put an end to his mother's damage once and for all.

Ten sanity-wrecking hours later, Jalal walked into the seafront house he and Haidar had provided for their mother in Aruba.

They'd picked the place based upon being as close as possible to Azmahar's climate, and the house to maintain the comfort level she'd been used to. In spite of everything, they'd wanted her to feel as at ease and at home as possible in her exile.

But it stopped here. His filial weakness. Not because he'd almost died when he'd thought Lujayn had been kidnapped, or because she'd sabotaged their wedding. It was what she'd done to Lujayn, again. He hadn't forgiven her for her past transgressions. Now, he never would. He couldn't bear to imagine Lujayn's anguish when his mother had forced her to leave their wedding.

Ya Ullah, how had she done it?

Waving away the guards he'd assigned to his mother, he strode into the one-level sprawling house with the first rays of dawn. The thought that she could sleep after she'd ruined his wedding, maybe even his life, had blood roaring in his ears, louder with each step closer to her bedroom.

"…everything you wanted."

The words barely carried to him, but they felt like a direct blow to his heart. For he didn't have any doubt who'd said them.

Lujayn. She was here.

His feet almost left the ground to home in on her voice. Then he exploded into his mother's private quarters, stood at the door staring at a sight he'd never thought he'd see. His mother sitting relaxed with Lujayn over steaming cups of tea.

Neither woman reacted at his entry. As if they'd both been waiting for him. His mother, in an emerald satin dressing gown that reflected some color onto the steel of her eyes, looked as majestic and ageless as ever. Lujayn, in a sedate gray pantsuit, had her hair still in the chignon she must have had styled for the wedding that never was. She kept her face turned away.

He had to tell her she mustn't feel bad, that he was here to…

"I'm glad you're here, *ya helwi.*" His mother's expression and voice were calm as she extended a hand to him. "Come, join us for tea. Or did you have enough stomach-turning beverages on the plane?"

His teeth gritted. "No, you don't, *ya ommi.* You don't 'my sweet' me. Ever again."

His mother gave a theatrical sigh. "*Zain,* let me get to the point without any…sweetening. Lujayn has always been my mole."

Everything went still. Had she just said…?

Incredulity and fury overcame him, crackled from his depths. "*Ya Ullah,* is there no end to your surprises? Why not tell me Lujayn is actually a man? That would be more believable."

His mother's gaze maintained its unwavering serenity. "I sent her to you when you were establishing the New York branch of your business. I needed someone I controlled to keep you away from the unsuitable women swarming around you, by giving you everything you needed from a woman with seemingly no strings and no price. But when you kept going back to her for years, I realized my plan had worked too well, was afraid you'd gotten attached to her. So I ordered her to start alienating you. But contrary boy that you are, you liked her more for it. I waited almost two years for you to walk out, but you didn't, so I ordered her out of your life, told her she could go for the other man she'd been… cultivating. Lujayn obeyed, of course, cut you off and married your friend, who was conveniently dying. I decided it was safer from then on to drive women away one at a time. But we know I haven't had to do a thing. You did it on your own ever since."

Jalal could only gape at his mother, his eyes flitting every other sentence to Lujayn. Lujayn's face remained turned away, what he could see of it was frozen, expressionless.

His mother went on. "While it was a relief at first that you wouldn't let anyone near, I felt worried, then guilty that I'd set you up to fall for my impostor, but hoped eventually you'd find others. I never predicted that you'd go after Lujayn after her husband died, wishful thinking on my part. I surely hadn't counted on you getting her pregnant. When she told me, I ordered her to stay away, hide the child. That is, until I needed to create a scandal for you."

Unable to feel shock anymore, Jalal only stared at his mother as she rewrote his whole history with Lujayn.

"But again, you, unpredictable boy, thwarted me. Before she could unleash the scandal of your illegitimate child from my servant's daughter, you had to go unearth her family's origins. While I was deciding how to deal with this new development and how best to use her child, you found out about him, jumped to acknowledge him *and* offered Lujayn marriage. So I told her to lull you till the last moment, then leave you standing at the altar. Now that the news has traveled the region, if not the world, no one in Azmahar will think that such a foolish man is king material."

No end. No end to the blows. To the injuries. He could have taken anything from an enemy. But from her…

His mother's face finally displayed an emotion as she rose in utmost grace to her feet, approached him with an entreating expression. "I love you, Jalal, but I want Haidar to be the king. Both of you forced me to take action when he stepped down and you kept going full force with your campaign. Now you're out of the running, he will take the throne. But he will make you his crown prince, and everything will be for the best."

Silence stormed in the aftermath of her heartless justifications. Jalal closed his eyes for several minutes.

When he finally opened them, they felt lined with sandpaper. Just like his throat and his heart when he looked only at his mother and said, "I don't believe a word you said."

His mother sighed. "As I expected. But you would believe Lujayn. Go ahead, ask her."

"What good would that do?" he huffed bitterly. "She'd say anything you want her to say, because she knows you'd carry out the threats that forced her here."

His mother inclined her regal head at him. "That's a very fascinating theory, *ya helwi*. What did you decide my threats involved? Harming her family? How would I do that from my exile?"

"Spare me, *ya ommi*. We both know you're here but your influence remains at large. Something I'll be rectifying from now on. And I will no longer have any qualms about employing my brothers' and father's help in severing your tentacles. So I hope you enjoyed abusing your power for the last time in your life."

"If you believe using my power to do what needs to be done is abusing it, then I was right and you're not fit to be king."

"You always hated me because of my Aal Shalaan face, didn't you? Just looking at me reminded you of your hated enemies, my father and his sons."

She shrugged. "I admit, looking at you is unsettling, but you do have parts of me, and you're my son. You're one of two people I love in this world. But I do feel more intensely about Haidar."

Bitterness almost overwhelmed him, when he'd thought he'd long come to terms with this fact. "*Aih,* the true part of you."

"All parents have preferences. I'm only honest about mine."

He looked at the mother he loved in spite of everything and wondered. Where did this endless well of emotion come from when it should have dried up decades ago?

He shook his head. "I long believed that Haidar is the loser between us, being your favorite. But I should have realized your lethal focus on him is a multiedged weapon, since you'd destroy anyone for him, even your other son."

His mother sighed, nothing on her flawless face courting his approval or forgiveness, just his understanding. "It's a matter of simple pragmatism, *ya helwi*. I love you and you will make a fantastic second in command, but he, the one with an Azmaharian face and a Zohaydan name, will make a better king for Azmahar."

"You thought he'd make a better king with that face for Zohayd *and* Ossaylan. You just want him on a throne so why even try to justify it? You want what you want, and you plot to get it, regardless of any devastation you may cause. This is exactly why I tried to keep my relationship with Lujayn a secret, fearing your ingenious manipulation, what you will always rationalize as necessary for the eventual greater good, and collateral damage be damned. In this instance, *years lost* when I could have been with Lujayn, with my son. You almost cost me and them our happiness together."

His mother tutted. "So you in one breath admit to my ingenuity yet still persist in thinking you had anything with her that I didn't manipulate you into? Why don't you just admit it and move forward? Tongues will wag for a while, and you won't become king, but you will be crown prince...."

"You talk as if Haidar and I are the only candidates."

His interjection had her eyes widening as if he'd said something too ridiculous to answer. She decided to humor him, it seemed. "You are the only valid ones. Rashid Aal Munsoori is damaged goods. Nobody in his right mind wants that unstable creature in control of anything, let alone a kingdom. Please, Jalal. He has as much chance as an iceberg in Azmahar's summer desert."

He had to laugh. "You have it all worked out, don't you?"

She nodded graciously. "I've said it before, and I'll say it again. You will *all* thank me later."

He shook his head again, unable to wrap it around the scope of his mother's capacity for deviousness. *Ya Ullah,* what a crushing shame she used all that insight and intelligence in such evil, world-scrambling pursuits. Was there any way to defang her, reroute her capacities to doing good, or should he just give up?

Give up, everything inside him said. He listened this time.

He circumvented her, walked to the frozen Lujayn. She didn't look up even when his legs touched her spastic ones.

"My mother's account provides a neater explanation for everything we had than anything I believe happened."

Her stiffness increased, her breathing stifled. Her face remained turned, eyes downcast.

He went down on his knees before her.

A gasp escaped her as his hands caught hers, keeping her in place when she tried to bolt away. She still wouldn't look at him.

"But what she didn't count on was one thing. That even if my version of what happened fits nowhere as perfectly as hers, even if she brings me evidence that it had all been another of her long-term plots, *I* know what's real. *You*—" he dragged her shaking hands to his lips then tugged her into a convulsive embrace "—are my only reality, *ya rohi.* You and Adam."

She looked at him then, and the force of her desperation detonated in his heart. Tears poured from her eyes as if under pressure, her voice a choked tremolo. "I can't be your reality. But she might let Adam remain in your life, if I am not."

"You will both *be* my life, for the rest of it."

She escaped his embrace, shaking all over, tears splashing his chest. "She won't stop at anything to drive me away from you. She believes she's doing you, and even Adam, a favor."

"She won't be able to do anything. I'll protect you and your family. I will never let her hurt you again."

"You think…I'd care if she threatened…to hurt me or my family?" Lujayn's sobs rose, chopping her words, as if each tore something inside her. "What worse…injury could she inflict on me than…losing you? As for my family…she's done the worst she could do to them already…knows she can't do worse…ever again."

"Then what is she holding over your head? Who is she threatening to hurt?" The ugliest suspicion that had ever assailed him tore into his mind. "Adam?"

And she cried out, *"You!"*

He staggered back on his heels, rocked to his core.

Too much. This was just too much. The blows his mother kept hitting him with. Was there no end?

Lujayn wept openly now. "She told me…she'd…destroy you. She said if I defied her and carried on with the ceremony, if I even told you, that she would, no second chances. And it wasn't…a threat. It was…a promise. I believed her. I—I still do. I came…to try to reason with her…but it's no use."

He turned a gaze numb with shock to his mother.

Exasperation tinged her exhalation. "You believe her?"

"I would believe Lujayn over my own eyes," he said, the words spontaneous, certain, his voice disembodied.

His mother's gaze hardened. "That only proves I was even more right than I thought. Now that I know how deeply she has you in her thrall, I *will* do anything to stop you from surrendering your name and honor to her. And to her family, who'll make you theirs, no longer your own person or your family's. Or mine. If you were in your right mind you'd know that no one in Azmahar will ever accept her family, reinstatement or not. If you think prejudices ever go away, then you know nothing about the people you want to rule.

"But the worst of it remains on her. No one will accept an unnatural union between a man descended from pure

royal lines on both sides with a mongrel slut who exposed
her body for the highest bidder. A black widow who you
claim married you during her husband's mourning period,
but who everybody knows is guilty of worse, of having illicit sex with you during that forbidden time, to trap you
with her illegitimate child." Steel blazed in her eyes. "But
the absolute worst of it is you. You're even worse than Haidar when it comes to giving your heart. I won't wait until
she pulverizes it. I'll destroy you first, before I see you destroy yourself. My destruction will be surgical, can be re-
constructed once I'm certain you're safe from her, not like
the infected mess she'd cause and that might necessitate an
amputation."

This time, as he stared at his mother, he wondered if he'd
ever find words again. *Ya Ullah*...that conviction that she
was ultimately doing this for his best.

His mother turned away, went to the open window where
dawn had conquered the night. "It's a simple equation, Jalal.
I have to be your eyes and your logic until both are working again. I might have let you wed her so you'd claim the
child, but when I learned you were leaving the *essmuh* in
her hand, that you were giving *her* the sole power to divorce
you, and control of your assets, I knew I couldn't wait for
you to wake up. You can claim your son, who does have
your blood, but her and her family, never."

Silence shrieked in the wake of her last words.

Then he finally pressed Lujayn's shaking hands and rose,
went to face his mother.

"Here's my simple equation, *ya ommi.*" He marveled at
how calm his voice was, how clearheaded he was. He knew
this would be his last effort where his mother was concerned. If she responded unfavorably, he would have no
mother anymore. "I won't say that inside you is a mother
who doesn't want to hurt her son, for I know I can't budge

you from your belief that you're saving me. But there *is* a mother who doesn't want to *lose* her son, even if he isn't her favorite, and a fool to boot. I know blood means everything to you, and you won't risk losing the third person you're equipped to love—your firstborn grandson. And you *will* lose me, and him, irretrievably, if you pursue this, and if you hurt Lujayn again, in any way. That isn't a threat. It's a promise."

His mother looked at him for what felt like an eternity, a lifetime of unsaid things passing between them, profound things he'd never dreamed existed.

Was that concession he saw in the depths of her eyes? Surprise? Even distress? Or was he just seeing the things he hoped to see?

But when she spoke her voice carried traces of all that, and dared he think, defeat, too? "*Zain*. I will back off."

Did that mean she feared losing him so much she would go against her nature? Could he hope?

Then she went on, and said nature was back, hale and hearty. "But you will come to regret your decision. Just pray it won't be 'irretrievable' when you do. And do promise you won't feel so foolish then that you won't come to me for help."

What do you know? The dragon lady *was* shaken. She'd gambled big and lost, was trying to scramble back to higher ground.

"I can tell you from now to not hold your breath, *ya ommi*." He suddenly did what not even he had expected, pulled her into a fierce hug. "But I can't tell you how much I hope that *you* one day will regret your actions, change your mind and make a new start. Think about it. Your family is growing, and instead of wary, infrequent visits from your sons, you can choose to connect with us all and find some peace and contentment."

His mother remained still in his arms. He knew it would be too much to expect an immediate response, and in front of Lujayn, too. Maybe never. But for his own sake, for Lujayn's and Adam's, he didn't want to harbor any bitterness toward anyone, starting with her.

He finally stepped away, hoping to get some reassurance from her. Her face was carefully empty, which told him more than any expression would have.

Then she gave him a slight smile, patted his cheek and swept away. There was majesty in her every move as she sat down on the couch, facing the frozen Lujayn, and rang a crystal bell.

"Might as well have breakfast," his mother said, looking at Lujayn as if she'd just met her. "Do you have any preferences?"

"Pinch me."

Jalal immediately pinched a handful of Lujayn's delightful bottom. She yelped then chuckled, still jumpy, her eyes dazed.

"I mean, your mother blackmails me into standing you up at the *ma'zoon,* then serves me breakfast half a world away? So, was this a hallucination? A breakdown?"

He grinned his love and relief down at her. "Whatever else she is, my mother thrives on being flabbergasting."

"Tell me about it." She melted deeper into his arms in his private jet's reclining seat as if she'd burrow into him, hide under his skin if she could. "Oh, God, Jalal, she was so convincing. *I* almost bought her version of what happened. As you said, it explained everything far more neatly than the truth. But you believed in me, against all damning evidence."

His hug tightened. "I did tell you I won't ever doubt you again. Turns out I not only won't, I can't."

Her giggle was almost delirious. "Sounds like you're under some hypnotic influence like your mother thinks you are."

"*Maa'loom,* for sure, I am enthralled fathoms deep with no desire whatsoever to ever resurface."

She squeezed him, her eyes filling with tears and reciprocation and they fell into a silence full of communication and communion.

Suddenly she jerked up. "God…your campaign! Will you be in a weaker position as a candidate now?"

"You mean because I couldn't even rule my bride?" At the pure mortification on her face, he couldn't help it and laughed his joy out loud. "*Aah, ya habibati,* I can't tell you how…*irrelevant* this is to me." Now she sputtered, her color dangerous. "But just to alleviate your misplaced guilt, all the drama, contrary to what my mother said, will probably boost my image, especially with women and younger people. We'll be an even more memorable romantic couple and our *matrimonius interruptus* will become the stuff of new-spun legends. Not that a popularity poll should decide what's best for Azmahar. But I'm not about to let the throne go, to anyone. Even had I wanted to, Haidar wouldn't forgive me if I didn't give it my all like always, and Rashid, after that stunt he pulled with you, has one hell of a fight on his hands. And may the best man win."

"*You.* You're the best man on earth!" Her kiss was fierce with everything inside her heart. "And I'm right there with you in any fight. I'd fight the very devil for you, for our future and our son and our happiness."

He guffawed. "You already did when you walked into the dragon's den to have that showdown."

"One I lost," she groaned. "You're the one who bailed us out."

"No, *you* did. The woman she thought you were would

have gone ahead with the ceremony and either told herself that my mother wouldn't truly hurt me, or assume I could protect myself. That woman would have let me deal with any fallout after she'd secured her place and interests. By complying, and going to her at that exact crucial time, you proved you love me so totally you'd give me up to protect me. I bet that messed up her projections, forced her to re-calculate. Then she saw for herself how clear and certain I am in my love for you, how I trust you so totally, and that must have reinforced the new realization that there's more to you than she thought. It's the real reason she backed down. I do believe she was trying to do what was best for me, and if she'd still suspected you were after my money or power, she would have taken me apart to get rid of you. So you, and only you, won that fight."

Wonder was rising in her eyes as he spoke, but with his last words, distress replaced it again. "I don't feel so tri-umphant when I remember... Oh, God, what are we going to do? The scandal I caused, no matter the reason—which we can't ever share—was witnessed firsthand by a thou-sand guests of the region's nobility and royalty and *God*... your family!"

He just smiled serenely. "We'll just gather them again tonight and have a do-over."

"Tonight?" Her face was the image of shock and dread.

"*Khair'ol berri 'aajeloh,* the best good is swift. Most of the menu is still edible and everyone remains in Azmahar. If they dispersed across the region, getting them back would be quite a chore, especially if they demand they'd actually witness our nuptials with a no-surprises guarantee before they return."

She buried her face in his chest, tears flowing again. "I don't know how I'll ever face anyone in Azmahar or any of your family again."

He smoothed her hair, soothing her. "Once my family knows everything, you'll be their favorite heroine. As for anyone else, who cares? They'll love you, or they don't matter."

"They matter to you. That's all that matters to me."

"Why don't you play that little recording I made you? Just to refresh your memory about what matters to me?"

Her hug was almost bruising this time as she mashed herself against him. "Ah, *ya habibi*...I can't ever tell you how I felt as I was taking off that dress, as I was leaving the palace and Azmahar, as I imagined what you'd feel when you found me gone. Every mile I traveled was dragging my soul out of me, as it refused to leave you. And then I thought there was no way I wouldn't lose you and I felt it snap..."

Needing to snap *her* out of her surrender to anguish, he tickled her. "First, no distance or plots or dragons will ever come between us. You'll never lose me, and I'll always find you, will always be with you, no matter what. Second, I suggest we head to the palace the minute we land. We'll dress up and sit in the *kooshah* and send everyone video proof of our presence there. We'll hold that miraculous miniature-palace cake hostage and threaten to demolish it if they don't come back running. How about that?"

She exploded in his arms, deluged him in kisses and laughter and tears. "Stupendous plan from my incomparable desert knight, owner of my heart and sharer of my soul...."

Laughing out loud, he took her roaming lips, stemming the flow of her adoration. "Save all those descriptions for the vows."

She rose over him, flushed with emotion, her eyes pulsing that hypnotic silvery glow, which he now knew only he triggered. "I'll never save any of it. I'll tell you now, and then and always. I'll show you and give you and love you with everything that I am, with every breath, for as long as I live."

Her conviction expanded in his heart, her devotion filled him to his recesses. Gratitude overwhelmed him that he'd been given so many chances to get this right. For this connection, this flesh, this being, everything she was—that was the reason for his existence. For everything.

He was saving that for his vows. Not because he didn't have more to tell her always, but because he wanted her to hear this particular confession for the first time as he proclaimed it to the world, as he claimed her and was claimed by her, forever.

For now, he gathered her, the flesh of his flesh, to him and whispered against her lips, "Deal, *ya hayati,* for as long as I live. And I'll raise you beyond life."

* * * * *

COMING NEXT MONTH from Harlequin Desire®
AVAILABLE OCTOBER 2, 2012

#2185 TEXAS WILD
The Westmorelands
Brenda Jackson
Megan Westmoreland has hired Rico Claiborne to uncover her family's history. But when their partnership turns personal, Megan discovers that passions burn hotter in Texas.

#2186 A PRECIOUS INHERITANCE
The Highest Bidder
Paula Roe
When a single-mom heiress and a loner hedge-fund billionaire come into conflict over the auction of a rare manuscript, will they find common ground...and true love?

#2187 A FATHER'S SECRET
Billionaires and Babies
Yvonne Lindsay
When a handsome stranger claims a mix-up at the IVF center might mean that her baby is *his*, this single mom could lose everything she values.

#2188 ALL HE EVER WANTED
At Cain's Command
Emily McKay
Ordered to find the missing Cain heiress, Dalton Cain must win the heart of the woman he's always loved but thought he could never have.

#2189 LOSING CONTROL
The Hunter Pact
Robyn Grady
Media mogul Cole Hunter needs to be in charge. But on an island location scouting trip, a new producer drives him to distraction...and into her bed.

#2190 WORTH THE RISK
The Worths of Red Ridge
Charlene Sands
Confirmed bachelor Jackson Worth is doing his family a favor by setting up sweet and vulnerable Sammie Gold in business...until the unlikeliest of love affairs blossoms between them!

You can find more information on upcoming Harlequin® titles, free excerpts and more at www.Harlequin.com.

HDCNM0912

REQUEST YOUR FREE BOOKS!
2 FREE NOVELS PLUS 2 FREE GIFTS!

Harlequin®

Desire

ALWAYS POWERFUL, PASSIONATE AND PROVOCATIVE

YES! Please send me 2 FREE Harlequin Desire® novels and my 2 FREE gifts (gifts are worth about $10). After receiving them, if I don't wish to receive any more books, I can return the shipping statement marked "cancel." If I don't cancel, I will receive 6 brand-new novels every month and be billed just $4.30 per book in the U.S. or $4.99 per book in Canada. That's a saving of at least 14% off the cover price! It's quite a bargain! Shipping and handling is just 50¢ per book in the U.S. and 75¢ per book in Canada.* I understand that accepting the 2 free books and gifts places me under no obligation to buy anything. I can always return a shipment and cancel at any time. Even if I never buy another book, the two free books and gifts are mine to keep forever.

225/326 HDN FEF3

Name	
	(PLEASE PRINT)

Address	Apt. #

City	State/Prov.	Zip/Postal Code

Signature (if under 18, a parent or guardian must sign)

Mail to the **Reader Service**:
IN U.S.A.: P.O. Box 1867, Buffalo, NY 14240-1867
IN CANADA: P.O. Box 609, Fort Erie, Ontario L2A 5X3

Not valid for current subscribers to Harlequin Desire books.

Want to try two free books from another line?
Call 1-800-873-8635 or visit www.ReaderService.com.

* Terms and prices subject to change without notice. Prices do not include applicable taxes. Sales tax applicable in N.Y. Canadian residents will be charged applicable taxes. Offer not valid in Quebec. This offer is limited to one order per household. All orders subject to credit approval. Credit or debit balances in a customer's account(s) may be offset by any other outstanding balance owed by or to the customer. Please allow 4 to 6 weeks for delivery. Offer available while quantities last.

Your Privacy—The Reader Service is committed to protecting your privacy. Our Privacy Policy is available online at www.ReaderService.com or upon request from the Reader Service.

We make a portion of our mailing list available to reputable third parties that offer products we believe may interest you. If you prefer that we not exchange your name with third parties, or if you wish to clarify or modify your communication preferences, please visit us at www.ReaderService.com/consumerchoice or write to us at Reader Service Preference Service, P.O. Box 9062, Buffalo, NY 14269. Include your complete name and address.

HDES11B

HARLEQUIN Blaze™
red-hot reads

Two sizzling fairy tales with men straight from your wildest dreams...

Fan-favorite authors

Rhonda Nelson & Karen Foley

bring readers another installment of

Blazing Bedtime Stories, Volume IX

THE EQUALIZER

Modern-day righter of wrongs, Robin Sherwood is a man on a mission and will do everything necessary to see that through, especially when that means catching the eye of a fair maiden.

GOD'S GIFT TO WOMEN

Sculptor Lexi Adams decides there is no such thing as the perfect man, until she catches sight of Nikos Christakos, the sexy builder next door. She convinces herself that she only wants to sculpt him, but soon finds a cold stone statue is a poor substitute for the real deal.

Available October 2012 wherever books are sold.

New York Times *bestselling author Brenda Jackson presents TEXAS WILD, a brand-new Westmoreland novel.*

Available October 2012 from Harlequin Desire®!

Rico figured there were a lot of things in life he didn't know. But the one thing he did know was that there was no way Megan Westmoreland was going to Texas with him. He was attracted to her, big-time, and had been from the moment he'd seen her at Micah's wedding four months ago. Being alone with her in her office was bad enough. But the idea of them sitting together on a plane or in a car was arousing him just thinking about it.

He could tell by the mutinous expression on her face that he was in for a fight. That didn't bother him. Growing up, he'd had two younger sisters to deal with, so he knew well how to handle a stubborn female.

She crossed her arms over her chest. "Other than the fact that you prefer working alone, give me another reason I can't go with you."

He crossed his arms over his own chest. "I don't need another reason. You and I talked before I took this case, and I told you I would get you the information you wanted… doing things my way."

He watched as she nibbled on her bottom lip. So now she was remembering. Good. Even so, he couldn't stop looking into her beautiful dark eyes, meeting her fiery gaze head-on.

"As the client, I demand that you take me," she said.

He narrowed his gaze. "You can demand all you want, but you're not going to Texas with me."

Megan's jaw dropped. "I *will* be going with you since there's no good reason that I shouldn't."

He didn't say anything for a moment. "Okay, there is another reason I won't take you with me. One that you'd do well to consider," he said in a barely controlled tone. She had pushed him, and he didn't like being pushed.

"Fine, let's hear it," she snapped furiously.

He placed his hands in the pockets of his jeans, stood with his legs braced apart and leveled his gaze on her. "I want you, Megan. Bad. And if you go anywhere with me, I'm going to have you."

He then turned and walked out of her office.

Will Megan go to Texas with Rico?

Find out in Brenda Jackson's brand-new Westmoreland novel, TEXAS WILD.

Available October 2012 from Harlequin Desire®.

HARLEQUIN®

nocturne™

Satisfy your paranormal cravings with two dark
and sensual new werewolf tales from
Harlequin® Nocturne™!

FOREVER WEREWOLF
by Michele Hauf

Can sexy, charismatic werewolf Trystan Hawkes win the
heart of Alpine pack princess Lexi Connors—or will dark
family secrets cost him the pack's trust...and her love?

THE WOLF PRINCESS
by Karen Whiddon

Will Dr. Braden Streib risk his life to save royal wolf shifter
Princess Alisa—even if it binds them inescapably together
in a battle against a deadly faction?

**Plus look for a reader-favorite story
included in each book!**

2 GREAT
NOVELS
SAME GREAT
PRICE

Available September 18, 2012

SPECIAL EDITION

Life, Love and Family

Sometimes love strikes in the most unexpected circumstances...

Soon-to-be single mom Antonia Wright isn't looking for romance, especially from a cowboy. But when rancher and single father Clayton Traub rents a room at Antonia's boardinghouse, Wright's Way, she isn't prepared for the attraction that instantly sizzles between them or the pain she sees in his big brown eyes. Can Clay and Antonia trust their hearts and build the family they've always dreamed of?

Don't miss

THE MAVERICK'S READY-MADE FAMILY

by Brenda Harlen

Available this October from Harlequin® Special Edition®

www.Harlequin.com

HSE65697